Unpopular Opinions 2

Unpopular Opinions Book Series, Volume 2

Taseef Farook

Published by Unfiltered Ink, 2025.

Table of Contents

Yaad | Prologue....................1
Sufi | Entry 1. Pride, greed, envy, and wrath....................3
Sufi | Entry 2. The cost of conformity....................21
Sufi | Entry 3. Purpose....................39
Sufi | Entry 4. Different lives....................57
Sufi | Entry 5. Scandal....................77
Sufi | Entry 6. Karma....................97
Sufi | Entry 7. My angel....................115
Sufi | Entry 8. All I had....................145
Yaad | Epilogue....................147

Copyrights Page

UNPOPULAR OPINIONS 2

By Taseef Farook

ISBN (paperback): 978-1-7638775-3-5

ISBN (Ebook): 978-1-7638775-1-1

Published by **Unfiltered Ink**

Adelaide, South Australia, 5000, Australia

Email: taseef@live.co.uk

Unfiltered Ink is an imprint of Dr Farook Ink.

Dedication

To my mother, who instilled the value of education in everyone she met.

Preface

I am an academic researcher and dentist with a unique cross-cultural perspective, having lived in Bangladesh, Malaysia, and Australia. My diverse background shapes the themes of this novel, as my experiences across these cultural landscapes deeply influence my writing. While all the characters in this story are entirely fictional, their struggles reflect real, systemic flaws in our society—issues that are often difficult to discuss. I believe that humour and wit provide the best way to navigate such sensitive topics, making them more accessible without diminishing their importance.

This book is my attempt to bring these stories to life, inspired by the many people who once shared their experiences with me and the lessons I have learned along the way. It is not written to criticise, but rather to highlight how far we have come and what still needs to change. Merging so many narratives into the voices of two protagonists was no small task, and I am deeply grateful to my partner, Lameesa Ramees, and my good friend, Ragib Farhat Hasan, for helping me weave it all into a singular, compelling story. I couldn't have done it without you.

Finally, I would like to thank Artificial Intelligence (AI) for proofreading my work. Yes, English is not my first language, and as a first-time author without the backing of a major publishing house, I couldn't afford a team of copyeditors.

Blank page

UNPOPULAR OPINIONS 2

Yaad | Prologue

"I AM F*CKED," I SIGHED, burying my face in my hands. "The bast*rd wrote things in his diary that make me feel like I should go back to Bangladesh, walk into a police station, turn myself in as an unwitting accomplice, go to trial, and plead insanity—because I still can't process how I got myself dragged into it!"

I was back in my counsellor's office after a year. He sat across from me, scrolling through his notes, clearly struggling to remember where we'd left off. "I wasn't expecting to see you again, Yaad. So... what did you find in your friend's diary?"

My eyes drifted to the cheap plastic hourglass on his desk. The sand clumped stubbornly at the neck, refusing to fall. Across the room, my counsellor was typing away on his keyboard furiously.

I tried answering his question while defending my deceased friend, fully aware that the contents of the diary could implicate a lot of people, including myself. "I found out that my closest friend had his reasons for what he did," I said carefully. "And now I understand why he went to such great lengths for me, teaching me so much about life. I just wish I could hug him and say thank you one more time."

But then, unable to hold it in any longer, I launched into a rant. "And you know what else I found out? My deceased friend was probably unhinged! *And* he was having these deep, thought-provoking conversations—with his inanimate diary!"

My counsellor gently interrupted, his tone calm but firm, he repeated his previous question. "What *exactly* did you find in that diary?"

I paused, inhaling deeply to collect myself. My hands instinctively fidgeted with the zipper of my bag on my lap, brushing against the top of the faux leather spine of Sufi's worn diary.

Sensing my hesitation, my counsellor looked at me and smiled. But it wasn't the comforting kind. It was the kind that made you feel like you were walking straight into a trap. "Read it for me," he said evenly.

2

Reluctantly, I pulled Sufi's diary out of my bag, set the bag on the floor, and placed the diary on my lap. I'd bookmarked the worst entries demonstrating Sufi's madness. Flipping to the first one, I hesitated.

"From the start, please," he interrupted.

I swallowed hard, nodding slowly. "Okay then... from the start."

Sufi | Entry 1. Pride, greed, envy, and wrath

DEAR DIARY...UGH, NO. I sound like some sappy romantic novel heroine. Let's try that again.

Diary,

Here's the thing: I think I'm handsome. Yeah, yeah, laugh all you want—my so-called friends certainly do. A**holes. But hear me out! If Edgar Allen Poe were to describe me, he might say:

"His face was a peculiar mix of boxy and soft, like a paradox made flesh—strong enough to stand out, gentle enough to invite trust. There was a certain calm about him, the sort of calm you'd want in a crisis. Even if the house was on fire, he'd probably say nothing useful, but his presence alone might convince you that burning to a crisp was just part of the plan."

Okay, fine. Maybe I'm not a "looker" in the traditional sense. Bite me.

Anyway, I was young, so cut me some slack. What I was good at, though, was chess. I loved playing with my mom—she always found a way to make it fun, even when she was obviously letting me win.

I should probably start writing more coherently, or tomorrow-me is going to be squinting at this mess, wondering if I was high on pot.

I have a twin sister, Sammy, who's three minutes younger than me. Sammy—she's the real prodigy in the family, poised to crush every academic record ever set. We used to joke she was just one award away from getting a full ride to Harvard. Petite and quiet, her oversized glasses screamed "genius in the making!" While our cousins loved dominating conversations, Sammy was content to sit back, soaking it all in from afar without having to make small talk.

My mom was this absurd mix of 'educated and unskilled' her whole life. She had degrees in English Literature and Psychology but spent her days as a housewife until we moved out. Dad was a government civil servant who had supported her in finishing her studies in English Literature—but with one ridiculous condition: she wasn't allowed to work. I know, it makes zero sense. Why bother encouraging her education if she couldn't do anything with it?

Back then, men seemed to want educated housewives—a sort of trophy with a degree to their name, but no job title. Personally, I want an educated *working* wife who'd support me, not the other way around. Then again, both of these mindsets feel a little off by today's politically correct standards, don't they?

Honestly, it made sense to me why she wanted to study English; it wasn't her first language, and there would be a sense of achievement in mastering it. But I always wondered about Westerners who were born with English studying English as a university degree. I mean, if you've been speaking it since birth, what's the point? Probably just an easy way to snag a degree and look smart while sitting on a pile of inherited cash or government debt.

Mom's side of the family wasn't wealthy, but they were honest-to-goodness academics. My grandmother—our *Nanu*—wasn't formally educated herself, but she made sure her kids were. Education and integrity were non-negotiable in her household. She had this secret rebellious streak, though. Mom always wanted to work, even though Dad had his ironclad "no job" rule. She wasn't afraid of Dad, he never hurt her. But what could she even do with a degree in English Literature? It's not like there were a ton of options in a rapidly industrialising Bangladesh, especially in the late '80s. If she'd been married to a rich guy, she might've been one of those "reinvented" trophy wives, claiming to be a work-from-home literary agent just to prove she wasn't entirely useless. Except Dad wasn't rich, so that pipe dream was a joke.

Even a decade later, with job prospects still slim, Mom never gave up trying. It became our little secret, and in exchange for keeping quiet, she'd read me English poems. She hoped it'd spark my love for learning, though she always nudged me toward "practical" fields instead of literature where success was exclusive to less than 1% of the population.

I figured it was her frustration talking—her struggles projected onto me. But deep down, I knew she just wanted me to have a secure future. One poem she recited often was Robert Frost's Stopping by Woods on a Snowy Evening. I can still hear her voice when I think of these lines:

"The woods are lovely, dark and deep,
But I have promises to keep,
And miles to go before I sleep,
And miles to go before I sleep."

Back then, job applications in Bangladesh were a hassle. Most companies had in-person submissions, and online job portals were still rare. Using them required a computer, which we had—thanks to *Nanu*—but mom was terrified she'd "break" it if she even touched it.

When Dad passed away from a heart attack last year, his infamous 'no job' rule came back to bite everyone in the ass. The only capable earner in the family—Mom—was left sitting idle, while the "inheritance" Dad left behind could barely cover a month's rent. As a government civil servant, he hadn't made it to retirement, so there were no pensions or retirement funds waiting for us. Turns out, dying early wasn't part of his office's plan. Shocker!

And then, just when things looked bleak, Mom stumbled upon a newspaper ad for a diploma course in computer science and programming. It was designed for total beginners—a novel idea for early 2000s Bangladesh. The cherry on top? The course offered a small stipend for candidates who completed the two-year program.

Back then, computer science wasn't the buzzword it is today. Only a handful of schools offered it as an optional subject, and universities weren't cranking out CS graduates like factories. Fast forward a few years, and now it feels like half the population has a CS degree doing call centre tech support jobs.

After talking it over with her siblings in academia, Mom decided to go for it. The entrance exam didn't test programming skills—it focused on IQ, English and Bengali language skills, and general knowledge. She borrowed study materials from the local library and prepared, although unsure if she could compete with younger graduates fresh out of school. But she was determined, and honestly, I think that's where I get my stubborn streak from.

A few more months later, Mom received a letter informing her that she had passed the entrance exam and was accepted for the course in computer science. How incredible! She had once been terrified of computers and was now about to learn to code programs herself! This represented a small glimmer of financial independence.

The initial plan to cut costs was to move in with my grandmother—our *Nanu*—who, coincidentally, lived in one of the sketchiest parts of town. In Bengali, we call our maternal uncles mama and maternal aunts khala. Mom's side of the family had plenty of khalas and mamas, each bringing along their crew of fun cousins.

Nanu lived in this house with a big open field in front. On weekends, some of my cousins would come over, and we'd play tag or hide-and-seek. That sprawling field made every game feel like an epic adventure. Meanwhile, the khalas would gather in the kitchen, cooking together or helping *Nanu* prepare the meals. When the food was ready, we'd all be called inside. A large cloth was spread out on the floor, and we'd sit together to eat—no fancy dining tables or etiquette nonsense, just good food and lots of laughter. I absolutely loved it.

But things had changed recently. *Nanu* had been forced to sell her beloved property to an influential politician who turned it into an extension of a hospital he owned. Sure, the land was taken under questionable circumstances, but at least it was for an ethical cause. I'll let you decide what you think about that.

Thankfully, she got a decent price for the property, thanks to my eldest mama, Azhar. A government official (and far more alive than Dad ever was), Azhar used his connections to negotiate a fair deal. It wasn't ideal, but was "a deal" to make the best out of a bad situation.

Now, let me introduce you to the family. Azhar was one of the smartest people I've ever known, but somehow, his culinary skills maxed out at offering omelettes or hard-boiled eggs to anyone who dared visit! In fact, only a few people I've met rival his intellect—one being his wife who was a painter and an incredible chess player! They had a son, who was a talented artist himself with a deep appreciation for the finer grasses of life... namely, marijuana – A man after my own heart! He had a habit of checking into rehab and lighting one up the second he checked out! He spent his days either locked away in rehab or on the roads with his painting equipment.

The middle *mama,* Mohfeez, was a medical doctor, always ready with a joke or two during our visits. He had lived and worked in Australia but grew disillusioned with the independence of Western life, where elderly parents are often left in nursing homes. He joked that children would abandon their parents at nursing homes, and the only time parents there get a visit is when the children come with a partner—an attorney to draft the will! Disillusioned by this lifestyle, he returned to Bangladesh, believing in the value of close-knit family and communal care. He even joked that in Bangladesh, a parent was more likely to be killed for the inheritance by their children than sent to a nursing home and patiently waited on to die! "Australians," he would say, "are polite and patient!"

The youngest *mama* used to be an "entrepreneur," an enterprising individual dabbling in various morally questionable ventures but never sticking to one. He ran with a political gang, but after being beaten up multiple times—by his own brothers, no less—he finally quit. His wife, a nurse, became his anchor as they moved far away to build a new life together.

As for my *khalas*, they were well-educated, worked nine-to-five jobs, and loved me dearly. Each of them had their own families, and I adored all my cousins who came out of these households. My mother's older sister, Mahima, was my mother's biggest supporter for every bad decision she ever made, including studying English Literature instead of Law, yes there was an option, apparently! Ironically, her daughter, Mahi, was the calmest presence in the family, the one we all turned to when we needed someone to confide in. Mahi had a way of making everyone feel heard, becoming the trusted confidant of all the cousins and was the first to welcome me with open arms after *Nanu*! My mother's younger sister, Yamina, is now perhaps the most accomplished woman in the family. Yamina went on to become a university professor and became an scholarly advocate for women's education. Yamina's daughter was Nessa, a rebel and a natural prankster and a bit of a menace! Sammy had this uncanny knack for silently trailing behind Mahi and Nessa, keeping just enough distance to watch their misadventures like a backstage observer. *Nanu* had a pretty big joint family living together under one big roof.

Nessa, Mahi, and Sammy got labelled the mischievous trio, though it was usually Nessa leading the charge into trouble. Mahi played the devil's advocate and was quick to defend Nessa's antics, while Sammy quietly tagged along, content to observe the chaos her sisters stirred up. Mahi had a passion for the literary arts, losing herself in books and stories (as a hobby, not profession!), while Sammy found joy in the natural world, fascinated by animals and the serenity of nature. Together, they balanced each other out—one the adventurer, one the voice of reason, and one the quiet observer, enjoying the ride.

If you're still with me after all these introductions, let me conclude by saying that we were in good company. Although at the time, my khalas and mamas weren't particularly affluent—most of them were still in the struggling phase of their careers—they taught me the value of perseverance and academic achievement. Though ironically, I still remained the dullest tool in that shed!

This stood in sharp contrast to the older generations on my father's side, who, steeped in generational wealth, couldn't have cared less about academic success. They held onto the outdated belief that girls should just marry financially successful middle-aged men as soon as they hit the age of consent. Practice what you preach, though—Mom ended up marrying a dud who struggled his whole life and voluntarily turned down promotions because he felt he was not worthy! The only reason my sister was even sent to school at that time was because my mom drilled into my father the idea that women should be educated enough to make their own bad decisions, just like the one Mom made by marrying Dad!

Our autorickshaw finally pulled up at the new place *Nanu* had rented in a downtown alleyway of Oldtown Dhaka. Mahi swung the gate open and waved the autorickshaw inside. On the porch, *Nanu* and Yamina stood waiting, their faces lighting up at the sight of us, while Nessa perched casually on the perimeter wall, waving enthusiastically as we rolled in. It was clear they had all been eagerly anticipating our arrival. Without wasting a second, *Nanu* hurried over to grab whatever bags she could and started hauling them to her room.

Mom, confused, interjected, "Ma, what are you doing?"

Nanu replied with calm determination, "I've decided Sufi and Sammy will take my room, and I'll move in with you."

"But Ma..." my mother began, clearly uncomfortable with the idea.

Nanu quickly shut it down, "Enough. Your food is ready. We'll talk about this after we eat."

And that was that. *Nanu* voluntarily gave up her room in the cramped rented house and moved in with my mother, all to make sure I was comfortable. She did everything she could to make us feel at home.

Later that afternoon, I decided to take a walk. Oldtown was a world apart from the nicer neighbourhoods—narrow streets and a labyrinth of alleyways, with street vendors on every corner. Building complexes were built so close together, almost all of them shared common walls with one another! Creepy individuals, teenagers, and street kids lounged around, smoking cigarettes and eyeing me in a way that made me feel like an outsider. Or maybe it was just my nerves. The place had a notorious reputation for political gang violence, and the proximity of the police station next door did little to comfort me. That part of Dhaka city had gangs menacing the streets in the same way shopping malls had its menacing pigeons—overestimating their ability to fly, refusing to give way to passersby, blocking cars like they owned the place, crashing into unsuspecting pedestrians, and then wobbling off as if nothing had happened.

Come to think of it, the intelligence levels were probably about the same, though the pigeons were a bit sharper—and definitely less violent. Ironically, I was never attacked by the gangs in Oldtown, but pigeons? They got me within the first few visits to the local shopping mall. People talk about ravens and magpies being territorial and aggressive, but trust me, pigeons can be just as much of a menace under the right circumstances!

At that time, exploring Oldtown or the surrounding areas wasn't even on my radar. I had only one mission: find an internet service provider. I needed broadband so I could chat with the two a**holes, Shiro and Rajesh, on MSN Messenger. Ads for different services were plastered all over poles and walls—something that would be considered pure vandalism in any developed country... yes, I keep up with current affairs. Despite how stupid I may look, I'm a well-read idiot!

The first ISP ad I saw, I jumped on it. I quickly saved the number in my phone, called them, and asked for the cheapest internet package they had. Locked it in, and then rushed back home, practically vibrating with excitement, waiting for some poor soul to show up and hook me up to the internet.

Now seems like a good time to clear up a few things. Diary, you're probably thinking, "A twelve-year-old boy, testosterone fuelled, must've been desperate for an internet connection to, you know, explore certain... content." And you'd be absolutely right—if this were one of those teenage dramas with vampires and werewolves. But this isn't that story. Back then, the only internet access I had was the dial-up I shared with Sammy, and by that point, I had already honed my "skills" the old-fashioned way—through imagination and art.

While my sixth-grade classmates were boasting about their newfound "anatomical knowledge" courtesy of the web, I quickly accepted that wasn't going to be an option for me. So, I took a different route: art class. Instead of pixelated images, I spent my time perfecting sketches of human anatomy—or at least what I thought it looked like. By seventh grade, I was a bit of a discount Picasso, obsessively sketching female figures in their birthday suits. Fingers, though? I could never get them right, so I'd just leave them out entirely.

Every day after hours of sketching, I'd erase the drawings in a panic before handing my artbook over to my mother for safekeeping. But no matter how much I erased, those faint pencil lines would still be visible—my seventh-grade brain soon realised that erasers were not magic. So, in a stroke of pure genius, I decided to cover the figures by drawing tornadoes over them. Yes, tornadoes—because what better way to mask "artistic expressions" than with chaotic swirls of destruction?

Page after page, I turned my artbook into a strange mix of unintelligible female anatomy and violent weather patterns. Eventually, Mom started flipping through it, confused, and I'm pretty sure at some point she thought, "Oh no, the boy's going to grow up to be a storm chaser!"

If you think *that* story is crazy, oh boy, do I have an even better one for you! Back in sixth grade, I signed up for two extracurricular courses: an art class—for reasons that should be pretty obvious by now—and a handwork class, under the firm belief that I'd be making clay sculptures of, well... let's just say, things that were also *obvious*.

Let me give you a life lesson: Read the fine print!

The first day I entered the after-school tutorial, I looked around and saw a class of forty girls and three boys. I thought, *"This is odd... but also inspiring. So many women want to make sculptures!"* Naturally, I took a seat in the far-back corner—exactly where a socially awkward boy would go in this situation. I watched as the two tutors at the front opened their stash, and out came... not clay, chisels, or hammers, but a piece of cloth attached to a loom and a threaded needle!

"Girls... and boys," one tutor began, "today we're going to do a simple line of stitch across the fabric." Instantly, all the girls...and boys... whipped out their own looms and threads while I sat there, utterly dumbfounded, staring at the hammer and chisel I'd proudly laid out on my desk. You'd think I'd storm out and never come back, right? Well, you'd be half-right. I did leave—but not for good.

That day, I went with my mother to the shopping complex and bought an assortment of coloured threads, looms, and fabrics. I came back the next day fully equipped. Why? Because when life gives you lemons, you stitch them into patterns and swallow them! The two other boys dropped out, but I kept going. By the end of the three-month course, I was weaving quilt covers while the girls were still struggling with pillow covers.

I even sold all my pillow covers at the student art fair. So yeah, I know how to paint *and* weave!

Okay, back to where I was.

The only problem was, we couldn't really afford much in Uttara, where we used to live. I had to save up just to get shish kebab from my favourite place. I could only afford it once or twice a month, and while that discipline wasn't necessarily a bad thing, it always felt a bit too restrictive. In my opinion, a child should be allowed to explore a bit—to taste life's offerings—so by the time they grow up, they already know what they like and don't like without wasting too much time. So, the first thing I did was blow my entire week's allowance on a shish kebab.

I was nervous at first. The first hour felt strange, like I was waiting for someone to tap me on the shoulder and tell me to stop, to go back home. But gradually, I started to feel something I hadn't before: freedom! I felt like an American just saying that! It was like I was in control of my choices, and that was exhilarating. I felt like crap afterward, though, because I had to walk back home and spend the rest of the week hoofing it everywhere. But hey, that's American freedom with debt! Buy now, pay later—literally. It was kind of like not wanting to wear a condom because it's more fun without it... and then regretting it for the rest of your life. Look at me sounding like a *sex connoisseur* without ever even bedding someone!

The good thing about being in an older, smaller neighbourhood was that most of the food joints were cheap. The downside? I quickly learned that many places kept costs low by reusing cooking oil—a trick that left me feeling bloated and, on occasion, dealing with an upset stomach. But hey, the food may have given me digestive regrets, but it also gave me a taste of freedom, and at that moment, nothing tasted better.

The money *Nanu* got from selling her property was split among all siblings, so my mother also received a share. While it wasn't a fortune, it was a good start. With that little financial cushion, she could afford to spend some on the food I enjoyed, which was a nice change of pace. After a while, I started to appreciate the smaller, albeit somewhat dangerous, neighbourhood. The streets were filled with business-minded people who had little to no education, and they seemed to pass on that entrepreneurial spirit to their children, often encouraging them to go into business instead of pursuing an education. While most were lovely individuals, some entrepreneurs did give off a "used car salesman" vibe where you'd be afraid to walk past their shop as they will try to grab your attention and not let go!

As I explored the area, I realised that there was a crowd for every type of person in Oldtown and its surroundings. The problem? I had no idea how to figure out which crowd was "right" and which wasn't! This was all new territory for me.

Later that evening, Mahi stopped by to see how I was settling in, with Sammy trailing closely behind her. They both hopped onto the bed facing me, eyes bright with excitement, eager to chat. As we settled in, I couldn't help but confess, "I feel really guilty about taking *Nanu*'s room." Mahi laughed softly, brushing it off, but Sammy's eyes twinkled with understanding as she was sharing the room with me.

Mahi smiled and reassured me, "*Nanu* loves you very much, and we're all really happy you're here. She would've been upset if you hadn't accepted her offer."

She then asked what I liked to do after I finished my homework. I told her I usually hung out with my sister or played video games.

Sammy chuckled as she turned to Mahi and said, "I'm not great at video games, but if you ever need someone to talk to, I can try to listen and interact!"

Mahi quickly chimed in, "Turns out Sammy knows all sorts of things about plants and animals. What do you like to do? I love reading books."

Her kindness caught me off guard. I asked, "Would you like to play chess?"

Sammy teased, "Yeah, but you need Mom for that. Chess makes my brain hurt!"

Mahi reassured Sammy, "That's okay! I'm not great at it, but I'd love to play if Sufi promises to go easy on me!"

I agreed, and we started a few rounds of chess, all of which I lost intentionally to show my appreciation for their kindness. While Mahi remained oblivious, Sammy saw right through it, smirking with every unusual checkmate I allowed myself to fall into.

Mahima and Yamina stayed over and offered to spin stories with me or whip up any dish I fancied, doing their best to make me feel at home. It was heartwarming—each of them had their own way of trying to make me comfortable.

Right around that time, an Internet Service Provider (ISP) official showed up at our place with a box of optic fibre cables. He measured the distance from my computer to their nearest tower box and stretched the cable all the way across. The problem with this setup, as I quickly learned, was its vulnerability to the elements—and the occasional hooligan who thought it'd be fun to cut a random wire draped over a wall in the alleyway. My blazing-fast 5kbps internet (yes, that's sarcasm) was often brought to its knees by rainstorms or a local teenager's outburst in the alley after going through a bad breakup!

Regardless, it took the providers a few hours to activate my connection, and by the next morning, I was online. The first thing I did was log into MSN Messenger and message Shiro, "how r u?" Yes, this was when abbreviations were cool—the only thing cooler was "sup?"

But don't worry, Diary, I'll spare you from any more. He replied almost immediately,

"Listen, your Aunt Jenny dropped by asking about your whereabouts."

Jenny was my dad's older sister—his own flesh and blood—and we were terrified of her. Every time she visited, she'd go off about how pissed she was that my dad would inherit twice as much of their paternal estate when they died, while she'd only get half because she was a woman. She'd constantly rant about women's rights and how unfair the world was to her, despite never having to lift a finger her entire life. She'd treat Uncle Naser, her husband, a moderately successful businessman, like dirt—belittling him every chance she got when he offered to help, calling him sexist and misogynist for not letting her do anything. And then, she'd complain about no one helping her, screaming that patriarchy was out to get her. You'd have to wonder if she'd be screaming about women's rights if her own son grew up and married someone like her. Safe to say, Sammy and I were fed up, while my mother called her a pathological liar and was terrified because Jenny was volatile and unpredictable.

Jenny never liked Mom, but she loved living for free at our grandparents' estate. Oddly enough, she was more upset when Dad died—not because of losing her brother, but because his death triggered a change in the estate's ownership. Our grandparents transferred the deed to Sammy and me, wanting to ensure we always had a place to live after losing our father. Jenny, who lived there with Uncle Naser, panicked at the thought of being evicted.

The estate was a kind gesture from our grandparents, but it was far from the city and lacked basic resources, making it impractical to hold onto. The logical solution? Sell it. And who better to buy it than Aunt Jenny, right? The problem was that she felt the estate was rightfully hers and did not want to pay for it. Although I suspected the real reason was she couldn't afford it—Uncle Naser had suffered two consecutive bad years at the fisheries. Jenny was terrified. She feared Mom would make us, as minors, transfer the deed to her name and sell the estate to someone else.

But here's the thing: Mom was never after money. All she wanted was education and financial independence for Sammy and me. She never had any intention of selling the estate until Sammy and I were adults, leaving the decision up to us. And just between you and me, Diary—I wouldn't mind having Aunt Jenny as a lifetime tenant, as long as she paid her rent on time! Jenny, however, couldn't shake her fear of being evicted. Mom always said that properties turn family into enemies, and I think she was afraid that might happen to us.

I darted a message at Shiro, "What did you tell her?"

Shiro panicked, "Nothing, man, nothing! Just said I hadn't seen you in a few days, but that's normal—like, you just disappear sometimes."

As Shiro and I chatted on MSN, Mom's phone started ringing nonstop, and she just let it ring, not picking up or even muting it. It was Jenny, of course. You could tell she was terrified—frozen in place. After about thirteen missed calls, one of my *khalas* gently urged her to answer, reassuring her that everything would be okay. As brave and daring as Mom could be, she was also easily frightened and had this tendency to freeze in place. Honestly, if you scared her in a kiddie pool, she'd freeze and drown!

Reluctantly, Mom picked up and put the call on speaker. To everyone's surprise, instead of anger, Jenny's voice sounded cold and authoritative.

I stayed quiet, my door cracked just enough to listen without giving myself away. Aunt Jenny's voice over the phone turned icy, flat. "I know you're the mother, but you're not in a position to look after them, my dear. Send them over to us—we'll handle them and their schooling. Naser's fisheries are doing quite well."

Mom protested, insisting she was perfectly capable of taking care of us, but Jenny hung up before she could get a word in.

Mom was too kind for her own good. She had power of attorney over the estate and could have used it in that conversation to bring Jenny to her hypothetical knees. But Mom would've called that blackmail—dishonourable and beneath her. She'd rather be a punching bag than deliver a blow herself. Sometimes, I wonder if we're even related!

I watched Mom, trying to hold it together, teetering on the edge of tears. Then, she turned to Sammy, who was standing next to her during the call, and said, "I'll take you and your brother to a few tutors—ones I can afford and think will help. Once I get a stable job, I'll get you two back into school" Sammy nodded without saying a word, and the next day, they spent hours visiting tutors, collecting their business cards so we could decide later that night.

The next evening, as I lay on my bed, flipping through brochures from the private tutors we'd visited, Sammy's phone rang. It was Aunt Jenny. I didn't know what to expect—half of me braced for a scolding, while the other half was overwhelmed by that sinking feeling, questioning why I had ever been born! Dramatic, I know. But as the phone rang, I quickly reminded myself it wasn't our fault.

I guess we took too long rehearsing what to say because the call went to missed, and since we didn't have voicemail, it just showed as a missed call. For a moment, I felt relief—until the phone rang again. Sammy picked up and held the phone in the air over her face in loudspeaker, unable to say a word. Her heart was probably pounding in silence. Then, to our surprise, Jenny said something I couldn't have prepared for!

"Sammy, are you settling in okay?"

Caught off guard, Sammy's throat tightened, and she barely managed to squeak out a response. "Yes," she said, almost too softly.

"If you need anything, don't think for a second that I'd turn my back on you just because I disagree with your mother. Jenny quickly added, "Can I make a request? Please call me for at least two minutes every day so I can hear your voice and know you're okay."

Honestly, why would I want to do that? Why would anyone want to talk to her? As an excuse, Sammy said, "I don't have calling credit on my phone." We used prepaid sims that relied on top-ups, and calls were pretty expensive.

There was a pause. "Let me call you back in five minutes," she said, before hanging up. We were left sitting there, surprised at how understanding she seemed.

True to her word, she called back exactly five minutes later. "Check your balance," she instructed.

Confused, Sammy dialled the code, and sure enough, her prepaid balance had been topped up—substantially, enough to last a month even if she made three-hour calls every day to friends she did not have! It felt a bit over the top, but I couldn't deny Sammy appreciated the gesture.

"I see the funds," she said, breaking the silence. "You didn't have to do that, but thank you."

"Anything you need, let me know," Jenny said.

I could see that Sammy felt a little more at ease as she replied, "Of course."

"Remember, call me every day, at any time. I guarantee I'll pick up. If I don't, I'll call you back."

"I will," Sammy promised, and the call ended. Obviously, the top-up had bought her attention, but sue me—we were kids who were always out of balance, and having some extra credit felt good! It didn't matter where the money came from.

Sufi | Entry 2. The cost of conformity

DEAR DIA-... NO.

...

We had a routine. I'd wake up late, have breakfast with Sammy while Mom was already gone—she had started attending her diploma course classes, so she'd leave early. *Nanu* would make food for us, and after eating, Sammy and I would study for a bit before finding ways to kill time together. In the afternoons, I'd get ready and head out to my tutors' houses, one after another, always alone. I'd grab my bag, step outside, and hail a rickshaw to their doorsteps. At first, the freedom felt exhilarating, but it quickly became monotonous and mundane within a week. Still, Sammy and I had no complaints. We had complete autonomy, which was a luxury in itself.

while me? I was the guy who'd probably fail at watching paint dry. Sure, I had a ton of knowledge, but it was all surface-level—flash with no substance. It's like I was the walking advertisement for capitalistic marketing: look good, sound smart, but have nothing of value underneath! I was good with words, so I studied commerce, while Sammy, who actually wanted to do something with her life, studied Science. Naturally, this meant we needed different tutors, and my "lack of ambition" (as Mom liked to call it) wasn't helping.

If Sammy's classes ran late and it started getting dark, Mom would come to pick her up. She knew the area wasn't the safest, especially for someone as "gullible and trusting" as Sammy was at the time.

In the evenings, I'd watch Sammy call Jenny for the hypothetical two-minute conversations, which often stretched into 30-minute sessions where she did most of the talking. she'd talk about her day, how she successfully raised her own children, and how much she loved Sammy. Some days, she'd repeat stories she'd already told Sammy; other days, she'd share something new. Pretty soon, the conversations became so monotonous that Sammy would phase out her words and carry on chatting doing her homework next to me as I chatted with the boys on MSN as she left the phone on loudspeaker.

Around the same time, Aunt Jenny started terrorising Mom. One day, Mom sat Sammy down, clearly exhausted, and told her that Jenny was gnawing at her, claiming that Sammy and I would be better off with her because Mom couldn't even afford our schooling. She cried, trying to assure me that she was doing her best. Sammy consoled her, saying she was perfectly happy with the private tutors and homeschooling—though the truth was, she wasn't.

Private tutoring is a highly lucrative business, with most tutors either renting spaces or transforming their living rooms into makeshift classrooms. The goal was simple: accommodate as many students as possible to maximise hourly profits while keeping individual fees reasonably low. This approach naturally attracted a diverse range of students from varying backgrounds, creating an eclectic mix of personalities under one roof. The tutors constantly belittled Sammy for not participating in class, while the other students—mostly from lower-middle-class families—targeted her because the tutors had made a point of broadcasting that she came from an upper-class background. Naturally, you can't break someone like me, blessed with the "used car salesman" mentality, with a bit of petty banter. But sweet Sammy? She couldn't take it. Every night, she'd tell me how she'd earned a handful of nasty nicknames, all designed to mock our supposed "fall from grace." It was like they had a competition to see who could outdo the others in cruelty.

I know my sister, and in her defence, she was never snobbish—She simply didn't talk to them because she was socially awkward. She told me she actually wanted to, but their conversations rarely interested her. According to Sammy, they mostly revolved around objectifying women on the streets, bragging about intimidating 'rival gangs,' and indulging in gossip about who is sleeping with the tutor.

There's a saying that if you're the smartest person in the room, you're in the wrong room because you're not learning anything new. At some point, the other kids must have sensed this and assumed Sammy's silence meant she thought she was better than them. While it was partially true—she wasn't learning much from those interactions—She never called them out or mocked their intellect, or lack thereof. Yet, she found herself despised simply for keeping to herself.

Sometimes, they would try to push Sammy down the stairs as she left the tutor's third-floor apartment. At first, she thought it was an accident—maybe someone just lost their balance or tripped. But by the second, third, and fourth times, it dawned on her that these little sociopaths genuinely wanted to hurt her. Yet, she couldn't bring herself to tell Mom. It would have crushed her. So, Sammy came to me.

Naturally, I did what any loving brother with a questionable moral compass would do: I followed her bullies home, lobbed rocks at their windows, and introduced them to the business end of a cricket bat whenever I caught them alone. It earned me the title of "trouble-maker," a badge of honour that spread through the neighbourhood faster than a celebrity scandal. But here's the thing about violence—it's like playing whack-a-mole. Shut one loudmouth up, and another group of pests pops up to take their place. Violence doesn't solve problems; it just presses pause on them.

Eventually, Sammy stopped telling me things. I guess that's on me. I should've been more mature—more diplomatic in "negotiating peace on her behalf," as she liked to put it, with an air of sarcasm that could've melted steel.

Sammy thought she'd made a friend in her tutoring class. She told me her new buddy's father had been a government official and knew Dad. That little detail seemed to mean something for Sammy—maybe she thought it gave them a tragic, cinematic connection or something.

After class, if it ended before nightfall, this supposed friend would walk Sammy partway home, stopping at an intersection where she'd join me because, let's face it, I wasn't about to let my baby sister wander too close to hooligans like myself. According to Sammy, the guy mostly droned on about sports and random hobbies while she nodded along but said nothing because she enjoyed his company.

Thankfully, they never exchanged phone numbers or chatted over the phone. I might've had to step in with my cricket bat again! But during those walks, Sammy genuinely believed she'd found a friend. It was almost adorable—like watching someone pet a stray dog, blissfully unaware it might have fleas.

Occasionally, this so-called "friend" would ask Sammy about our family, and because she's Sammy—sweet, trusting, and just a little too open—she'd share bits and pieces. One day, when the little opportunist found out she was living with Mom alone and had stopped going to school as part of our strategic cost-cutting measures, the jerk decided it was time to flex his inner armchair psychologist. He told Sammy she was dysfunctional and broken. Dysfunctional and broken! I mean, who even says that to a thirteen-year-old? Naturally, Sammy cried her eyes out, and I wanted to give him a one-way ticket to Bat Land, but she made me promise not to. I agreed—grudgingly and under protest, of course.

Over the next few weeks, Mr. Judgmental Genius began to distance himself. It was painfully obvious he wanted nothing to do with Sammy anymore. Why? Because she'd confided in him about her family's struggles. sharing stuff like that is applauded—it's all about "normalising vulnerability" and "mental health awareness." But is it really? It is like handing someone a juicy piece of gossip wrapped in a bow. People don't want to listen so they can understand; they want just enough material to spice up their lunch break conversations.

Sammy was too naive to see it coming. She thought openness would bring empathy, but instead, it brought judgment. It's like those people who ask, "How are you?" but secretly hope you say, "Terrible," just so they can feel better about their own lives. Honestly, hypocrites like that are worse than flying cockroaches—at least cockroaches don't pretend to care before scurrying off!

During this time, Sammy began failing every assignment her tutors gave her—not because the material was difficult, but because she was constantly bullied by other students, leaving her unable to focus on anything the tutors were teaching. She didn't have the courage to report the bullying, fearing it would only lead to retaliation from my tormentors and she stopped coming to me because I was hyper vigilant! As a result, everyone assumed she was struggling academically, completely unaware of the real reason behind her poor performance.

At our quarterly parent-teacher meetings, some of her tutors spoke to mom, telling her that Sammy didn't stand a chance of passing all eight subjects in her O'Levels exam, let alone succeeding in A'Levels with my existing performance. Diary, the O'Levels were the exams taken at the end of Year 10 before starting college, following the British curriculum, which many English-centric institutions in Bangladesh adhered to due to their colonial roots. The alternative was Bangla-centric institutions, where students took matriculation exams like the SSC for Year 10 and HSC for Year 12.

At some point, God knows how or when, Sammy confided in Jenny about the bullying she was facing and her failing grades. Jenny's only response was, "I don't think you should quit school."

"School is very expensive," she replied, referring to the one we attended in Uttara. She simply said, "It can be any school," which, in hindsight, seemed quite reasonable coming from Aunt Jenny. Sammy brought it up with Mom, and though she acknowledged it would be stressful, she agreed for once with Aunt Jenny that we could probably afford to enrol at least Sammy in one of the less expensive schools that followed the British curriculum.

Aunt Jenny, being rational and understanding? My a**! One weekend, a lawyer showed up at our door. Jenny had filed a lawsuit against not only Mom but her entire family, claiming that they were wrongfully keeping Sammy and me with them, despite their inability to financially support my needs. This lawsuit also meant that we could not accept any financial support from anyone associated with Dad's side of the family until the case was settled.

In hindsight, it was clear that Jenny had been playing the role of a military tactician, carefully dividing her opponents and turning them against one another. She kept up a good relationship with Sammy, slowly building trust, while simultaneously creating distance between her and my Mom and I. She ensured that my connection with Sammy was reduced to a minimal by calling me reckless and telling her that I was the cause of Sammy's bad fortunes. Bollocks! Eventually, Jenny painted Mom as the villain, casting herself as our only saviour, aka, Super Jenny! Sammy was too naive to see it then and too helpless to care, even when she did start noticing.

This lawsuit placed an immense strain on my mother and her siblings. Tensions ran high, and her family urged her to confront Jenny directly, in the presence of lawyers, to find out what exactly he wanted. Despite her struggles, Mom was always someone who could be reasoned with when approached properly, so she agreed. We hired a lawyer, a friend of Afzal, our eldest *mama*, who offered to do part of the work pro bono. When Sammy talked to dear Aunt Jenny, the lawyer suggested that Sammy asks her directly what his demands were, as the lawsuit itself was vague. It wasn't a clear-cut case of concern from a good Samaritan— It bordered on accusations of child abuse, seemingly designed to get my mother expelled from the diploma course she was undertaking. The course had strict character requirements, and if the accusations stuck, it would ruin her reputation, destroying any chance she had at building a career.

That night, like every other night, Sammy spoke to Aunt Jenny over loud speaker as I listened in. She mustered the courage to ask Jenny directly, "You filed a lawsuit against Mom, why?"

Jenny replied calmly, "I only want what is best for you, sweetie."

"But what do you think is best for me?" Sammy pressed, hoping for some clarity.

"You should not have to leave school," she said.

"We've already decided that we'll restart school," Sammy responded, trying to reason with her.

There was a long pause on our end, but Jenny quickly broke it with a chuckle, switching topics as if the previous conversation hadn't even mattered. "We're thinking of buying a new car. Do you have any recommendations?"

Caught off guard, Sammy hesitated before offering, "I don't understand cars as much."

Aunt Jenny responded almost immediately, "Let me know if you think of anything. I value your feedback the most."

She was clearly trying to buy her way into Sammy's life, and the worst part? I think it was actually working. Sammy, sweet and oblivious as always, was eating it up like free candy at a carnival. Meanwhile, I was sitting there, making every exaggerated hint I could think of—dramatic throat clears, wild hand gestures, even mouthing hang up!—but Sammy just kept shushing me like I was the one being unreasonable. The audacity!

While she framed all her conversations as attempts to help Sammy open up to her, I saw it for what it was. Encouraging vulnerability, promoting openness, yet weaponising that same trust when it suits their purpose. Some call it gaslighting: making the person who confided feel small or using their words against them. When women do it, society often brushes it off with clichés like, "Women! Can't live with them, can't live without them," as if this behaviour were exclusive to one gender. But the truth is, anyone is capable of it, and my society only seems to care when the gaslighting is done by the man.

In that moment, I could sense the subtle shift in Jenny's tone—from the caring aunt she had portrayed herself to be, to a self-absorbed person showcasing her ego and letting Sammy know that we were not doing as well as her. While I am sure Sammy could see through some of what she was trying to do, She had also grown desensitised to it over time. The frequency of their conversations had dulled Sammy's sensitivity to her manipulations.

I realised something that night: human nature conditions us to either favour or, at best, become indifferent to events we're familiar with—whether they're good or bad. Repetition can either strengthen us, like studying for an impossibly hard exam, or it can wear us down, like convincing a hostile board that you're the right person for the job. Consistency is key.

Sammy rejoined our old school in Uttara, braving the long, exhausting commute between there and Oldtown on the other side of the city by school bus. Meanwhile, Jenny and Mom were entrenched in what can only be described as a courtroom soap opera. Jenny wasn't subtle about her intentions—she made it painfully clear that there would be no financial support for Sammy's education through liquidating the estate, under any circumstance. Instead, she would postpone court meetings, hell-bent on stalling the entire process.

Her strategy was as transparent as it was diabolical: drown Mom in legal fees and emotional exhaustion. She delayed every hearing with the intention of dragging things out for months, even years, with new accusations being flung in like confetti at a parade. Just when one claim was on the brink of resolution, Jenny's lawyer would pull another rabbit out of the legal hat. At one point, the only charge left to slap on Mom was child abduction.

To make matters worse, Jenny snuck in a clause that barred Mom from switching Sammy's schools under any circumstances. The audacity of it! It was a calculated move designed to keep the financial noose tightening around Mom's neck. The goal was clear: bankrupt her into submission. Jenny knew Mom's family couldn't step in either; they were struggling themselves and had no means to fund a legal battle that seemed to have no end in sight.

It was like a slow, grinding game of chess, where Jenny's pawns blocked Mom's every move. She had cornered her with no rook, bishop, or queen left to defend herself, and Jenny's queen and knights were taunting her with every new legal claim. There was no escape, just a cruel waiting game. School became unbearably expensive for my mother, whose stipend could barely cover the costs. She was forced to dip into her savings—money from the land *Nanu* had sold. And on top of that, the expenses of court hearings and the emotional toll it was taking on her mental health were unbearable.

It was in that moment I realised just how deeply money—or the lack of it—could bring an honest, hard-working person to their knees. This wasn't a life lesson, just a painful observation.

Meanwhile, Jenny's lawyers forced Sammy and me to appear in court several times a month, claiming we weren't being looked after properly under Mom's care. The judge would ask if we were happy with the life we had. Before each hearing, Aunt Jenny would call Sammy and say, "I don't expect you to say anything on my behalf. Just be honest about what you're facing."

But Mom's lawyer warned that this approach would play into Jenny's hands. Any response would force both sides to reciprocate, dragging us into a prolonged legal battle that Mom couldn't afford. Even if she agreed to Jenny's terms in court, Jenny would impose absurd conditions—like giving up her education because Dad had once imposed a "no job" rule, which Mom technically consented to. Jenny knew neither Mom nor any judge would agree to this, and it wouldn't hold up in court. She'd reappeal, dragging the case on and pushing Mom toward financial ruin until she had no choice but to accept Jenny's terms. In essence, a tie was a win for Jenny. It was ironic how two women were now playing the game of "consent matters" in this twisted way.

So, each time we went to court, we said we were perfectly happy with our lives. We were hoping that it would at least help speed up the resolution of the case—It never did; Jenny's lawyers made sure of it!

Sammy had to skip school for every court date and meeting with the judges and lawyers, who were just as rude as the bullies at school to her—only with more education, making their insults more draining. Ironically, those were the days Sammy said she actually looked forward to being back at school, facing her favourite bullies instead!

Finally, Mom had enough of Jenny's antics, and the lawyers pushed for an out-of-court settlement to bring an end to the stupidity. After months of legal jousting, an agreement was drafted. So, what did Jenny demand from us in exchange for a truce?

Irrevocable Power of Attorney over our inherited estate, with a clause stating that she would remain the permanent caretaker unless Sammy and I unanimously decided otherwise. Even then, our decision would only be considered valid if at least one of us had received the "appropriate education" our dad had envisioned before his passing. In other words: no switching schools. Essentially, Jenny would hold the reins indefinitely, banking on the fact that sweet, kind-hearted Sammy would never ask her to step down. And let's be honest—Jenny wasn't wrong. Sammy's gentle nature made her an easy mark for her manipulation.

But Jenny wasn't just banking on Sammy's reluctance; she had a backup plan. If Sammy ever grew a backbone and decided to act, Jenny would immediately file a counter-lawsuit, claiming that the agreement had been signed under duress and I had coerced Sammy into it. Classic Jenny—always two steps ahead. Checkmate!

School became a whole new level of hectic for Sammy. I was privately tutored but Sammy had a hard time. While the morning commute across the city was bearable, the journey back was an entirely different story—humid, exhausting, and nerve-wracking thanks to the infamous Dhaka traffic. What should have been a 26-minute ride home stretched into an agonising 3.5-hour ordeal every day. Since we couldn't afford the air-conditioned school bus, Sammy had to deal with the scorching heat waves blasting through the open windows, making life even worse.

Attending school was supposed to be Sammy's biggest challenge, but the courses proved to be an even steeper hill to climb. Months of court battles had left her behind academically, and no amount of late-night study sessions could completely bridge the gap.

Sammy would share her day with me every night. "Everyone knows I'm socially awkward," she'd say with a resigned laugh, "so they mostly leave me alone." There was some teasing, but it was light-hearted—the kind they all dished out to each other. In a strange way, it was a relief for Sammy and for me too; at least she wasn't a punching bag.

But Sammy had it worse—attending a prestigious school while grappling with financial struggles added a new layer of social anxiety for her. She might as well have worn a neon sign that screamed, "Easy Target!"—like a flashing beacon for every bully within a kilometre, or roughly the length of 1,660 washing machines side by side, if we lived in America.

The truth, as embarrassing as it was, was that Sammy had fallen behind. We weren't well-off enough to afford both her school fees and the army of private tutors that every other kid seemed to have on their rich daddy's payroll. To compensate, Sammy began fabricating achievements, spinning tales about hobbies and awards she allegedly racked up outside of school. It was her way of keeping up appearances—a fake persona similar to the one a social media influencer might do with their online posts.

I kept warning her, "Sammy, people see right through this stuff. Just be yourself!" But she wouldn't listen. Her carefully constructed façade didn't hold up for long, and once her classmates caught on, she became their favourite punchline. What was supposed to be a protective mechanism quickly turned into a comedy act where she was the star performer, much to her dismay.

While she was among familiar faces in class, she also encountered new classmates—some of whom were less kind about her appearance during the awkward throes of puberty and crooked teeth. Unfortunately, she was often seated near them. If they cracked a joke and Sammy dared to smile, they'd turn to her and sneer, "That wasn't for you. No one wants to see that ugly smile!" Sometimes, one of them would smack the back of her head, and when she looked back, they'd mockingly say, "Every time I see you smile, I feel like beating you up."

Sammy finally opened up to Mom about the bullying she endured at school because attributing it all to her smile and crooked teeth. Mom was concerned, and instead of our usual quiet lunches and routine afternoons, she decided to take Sammy to a few dentists to explore her options. Sadly, the quotes Mom received were astronomical, far beyond what we could afford.

Two weeks later, Mom took Sammy and me when she went to visit a family friend. I didn't think much of it until we arrived at the friend's house, which, to my surprise, turned out to be an orthodontist's office.

The family friend was a kind orthodontist who understood Mom's financial struggles. She generously offered to fix Sammy's teeth for a minimal fee, one that barely covered her costs for materials and upkeep. Mom, though worried about managing the finances, looked at me and nodded in agreement. "I can always set aside some money from my stipend for Sammy. It's not like I have anything else to spend it on other than my two children!" she said with a faint smile. That evening, Sammy walked out of the office with braces on and a newfound confidence, knowing that in two years, she'd be able to smile without worrying about being bullied for it!

At school, things got worse once her fabricated stories of an affluent lifestyle caught speed. Sammy became the butt of their jokes. They'd bait her into retelling a lie she'd spun the previous week, only to laugh when her stories didn't line up. To her credit—or perhaps her detriment—Sammy dug her heels in, doubling down on her pretences.

I'll admit, even I'd occasionally feel like shaking some sense into her for the things she said!

I wasn't in school to intervene directly, so I asked Shiro and Rajesh to look out for her. This often landed them in trouble for stepping in to defend my baby sister. The bullies loved playing the victim card, whining to teachers and peers whenever Shiro or Rajesh pushed them away from Sammy—who, in true family tradition, froze in the middle of conflict just like Mom would. Soon enough, the bullies branded Sammy as "the thug's sister" and labelled Shiro and Rajesh as "his goons."

Nevertheless, Sammy transformed from a socially awkward child into an obnoxious teen, desperately seeking validation from peers who enjoyed the privilege of generational wealth to support their every venture—and every mistake. I don't mean to dismiss everyone in that circle; I know some amazing individuals who have accomplished great things with their parents' money, like studying overseas and securing great jobs. However, many of them used their family wealth just to get by, never quite living up to their full potential. They may be lovely people, but their privilege often overshadowed their true capabilities. But try telling that to my thirteen-year-old sister who was desperately trying to mimic their lifestyle!

Very soon, Sammy started failing her courses. The reality that she couldn't even justify her place at school—especially with Mom's extreme investment in her education—was sinking in. Sammy was barely passing one or two courses, and it became clear that education in South Asia is often more about rote memorisation than understanding the bigger picture. Teachers rarely stop to ask why a student is struggling, which is probably for the best—after all, there's no shortage of lazy students who would just abuse the system if they could. But it also means that genuinely struggling students, like Sammy, fall through the cracks because they choose to stay silent.

Sammy's biggest struggles were with Physics and Chemistry. So, she resorted to cheating, copying off her classmates' papers just to stay afloat. Every day, she'd come home and confide in me. She couldn't help it—she was a sucker for a confession, even though, in my opinion, the more you talk about a "sin," the more trouble you invite. Personally, I chose silence; less trouble that way. Except for with you, Diary, you're different!

Then, one day, she came home and cried to me. She'd been caught copying answers in her Physics exam. The teacher, instead of offering a calm word of reproach, physically punished her. He yanked her sparse sideburns and slammed her face onto the table. I was floored. This kind of behaviour from a teacher at a "high-end" school? Unbelievable. But then again, it explained why he was quietly let go afterward.

I immediately went to the principal's office, demanding the guy be charged. The faculty, predictably, defended the pr*ck, claiming the evidence was inconclusive because no student would testify. Well, no sh*t Sherlock! Who's going to risk their grade just to stand up to a teacher who can fail them in the final exam? But of course, the guy wasn't charged with child abuse. Why would he be? Allegations like that are typically reserved for people from "questionable" backgrounds—or media celebrities—not someone from a "well-respected" family!

Sometimes, you just have to take justice into your own hands. That night, I found myself planning a "retribution" mission—complete with a cricket bat and the usual backup of Shiro and Rajesh. Wrecking his car wasn't exactly the most thoughtful solution, but it sure as hell felt satisfying. Justice may not always be served by the system, but at least we could sleep at night knowing we gave it our best shot.

It became clear to me that Sammy wasn't exactly embraced by anyone at school, so I asked Shiro and Rajesh to keep a closer eye on her when she wasn't in class, just to ward off any bullies. Sammy liked hanging out with them, and it made me realise something important—people often think you can't have friends if you're socially awkward, but it's just harder to make new ones. And when those who understand you leave, it's like trying to float in an ocean with no lifeboats.

There was also another student in Sammy's class who had it worse. She was a recovering drug addict who was constantly bullied, and unlike Sammy, she didn't have the support of friends like Shiro and Rajesh. To keep her identity hidden, let's call her Frankie—an English name, fitting for a school where some students had names like John, Tanya, and Sarah. There's a belief in many Asian communities that giving your child a Western-sounding name will help them land job interviews in Western countries, where it's assumed the first screening is based on the name on the résumé. Diary, you can decide for yourself if that's a myth or reality!

One day, Sammy was sitting in Frankie's seat, chatting with the boys. Apparently, she wanted to share one last story with the boys. Frankie returned fidgeting and asked Sammy to move. "Fair enough," I thought, when Rajesh recounted the story to me later. But Sammy told Frankie to take her seat on the other side of the classroom for just a minute while she finished up. Shiro said that Frankie immediately snapped and demanded Sammy move right then and there. Sammy froze.

At that point, Shiro asked Frankie, "Is there a problem?" But Frankie didn't even acknowledge him. Instead, the b*tch started nudging Sammy aggressively, who was now apparently frozen in place out of fear. In a blink, those nudges turned into a vicious yank on Sammy's ponytail, sending Sammy and her chair crashing to the ground. On her way down, Sammy's left eye hit the sharp corner of the table next to her. Sammy's left eye sank into her socket, and her vision on that side went dark.

Dazed and stumbling, Sammy tried to make her way to the nurse's office, but she collapsed before she could get there, falling unconscious before Shiro and Rajesh got to her. The next time she came to, she was in the principal's office, with me holding her head in my lap. The office staff was trying to call an ambulance when she passed out again. When she woke up the next time, the damage was done—she couldn't see out of her left eye.

Both my mom and I lost it at the principal's office. We were demanding Frankie's family be dragged in front of us, and I suggested that Frankie should be kicked out of school for what she did. The principal, of all people, had the nerve to say, "I understand it's a grave situation, but I don't expect your kind to handle things with finesse. Both Frankie and Sammy were in the wrong."

I snapped back, "Excuse me? You're comparing being stubborn to being maimed in retaliation? Seriously?" Of course, I already knew the deal—Frankie was the daughter of some bigwig political figure, and the school wasn't about to piss off someone with that kind of influence.

It's like this all over the world—wars are fought, and armed, influential people are given a free pass for mowing down the unarmed just because of who they are. So what the hell is little Sammy supposed to be in the middle of all that? Just some collateral damage. The punishment should fit the crime, an eye for an eye, so to speak!

The school sent Mom a formal letter, condemning Frankie's actions as "reprehensible," but then tried to justify her behaviour by explaining she was going through some mental trouble at home and that Sammy's 'unjust' actions pushed her to the brink. The nerve of these people! They suspended Frankie, but as a nice little twist, they assigned Sammy to after-school community service to "teach her compliance." You couldn't make this sh*t up.

And the worst part? Sammy forgave Frankie! Sammy told me, "It's okay, I'm not completely blind, and I was in the wrong!" No, Sammy, you weren't. There are different levels of wrong, and what Frankie did was on a whole different scale. To make it worse, Frankie had the audacity to post on social media, "Showed her where she belongs!"

I'd had enough. I wasn't about to show her the business end of my bat—not because she's a woman, but because what she did was far worse than something a quick beat-down could fix. So, let's just say I knew a guy who knew Frankie's coke dealer. Yeah, turns out, she was an addict. I might've given the dealer a little tip-off, telling him Frankie was about to snitch on him and his bosses. See, every scum organisation has a hierarchy, and at the top is "saving your own a**." You make someone think it's in their best interest to do something otherwise their a** is on the line, and they'll do it.

A tabloid piece later reported on the daughter of a powerful politician who'd fallen into drugs and gone south in a bad deal. She was eventually found dead in a ditch taken out by a dealer over some unpaid debt. Naturally, this didn't hit the bigger news outlets, because it was too scandalous, and journalists were assassinated for exposing much less than this. Whether getting a drug addict off the streets is a "good" outcome or not, I'll leave that for you to decide, Diary. On one hand, she was someone who lost her way to drugs. On the other, she was a drain on society—someone who'd never change and would inevitably end up leeching off taxpayers while her family distanced themselves to save their own hides from the fallout.

Naturally, Sammy didn't take the news well, and it took some serious convincing to make her believe I had nothing to do with any of it. We lay on the floor, staring at the ceiling, while she told me stories. As brilliant as she was academically, she was humble and completely immersed in her love for plants and animals. Whenever she saw her audience start to drift, she'd effortlessly switch gears, diving into talks about cartoons and anime—most of which, unsurprisingly, also involved plants and animals. It was probably why she let Nessa or Mahi take the lead in conversations. Their towering figures would cast a shadow over her petite frame, and she'd hang back, quietly observing. I used to tease her, asking if she was hiding behind them like a human shield.

Despite her past accomplishments, Sammy led a simple, grounded life. She was refreshingly easy to talk to, though sarcasm usually flew over her head. She mentioned how she wanted to become a doctor—or at least earn a PhD—just to have the title and fool people into thinking she was important. I couldn't help but laugh, remembering how Sammy always made fun of Afzal for constantly bragging about his PhD while being utterly useless around the house. He had a knack for overcomplicating things and would endlessly ask, "So, what is your hypothesis?"

As we chatted, she slipped in some anime references I didn't quite get, but I appreciated the humour, finding it a welcome distraction from everything else happening around us.

After a pause, she asked, "How can I be more like you?"

I laughed. "A hopeless idiot who can't even count backwards from 10?"

She laughed," No, I meant charismatic—not socially awkward. You weren't always like this; what changed?"

I thought for a moment before replying, "I'm flattered by the exaggeration, but it took time and a lot of lessons to grow. Since you're interested, I can share a few things I've learned along the way. Better yet, I'll guide you through it, hand in hand, as I show you the different realities of life!

Her face lit up. "I'd love that, thank you!"

And so, I started telling her about some of my misadventures with Shiro and Rajesh—of course, leaving out the more colourful details for the time being. She wrapped her small hand around mine as she listened, squeezing it gently while her eyes grew heavy. Soon enough, she dozed off, her soft breath rising and falling in sync with the peaceful silence. I didn't need anything more than a pair of jeans and sandals to be content. Thank you, baby sister, for giving my life a purpose.

Sufi | Entry 3. Purpose

DEAR...F*CK! AGAIN!

...

Diary,

...

An entire year has passed since my last confession, and there's so much to catch up on. I skipped an academic year to help save on tutoring expenses so that Mom could focus more on Sammy, who had always been the brighter one.

Let's start with the big news: Mom landed a job as a programmer, and Yamina secured a tenured professor position at a university. Mahima, Yamina, and Mom pooled their resources together and bought a second-hand car—a beat-up Toyota Probox. It wasn't much to look at, but at least it ran. It was meant to be for the girls to use when they needed to get around, as public transport in Dhaka was still a hassle for women. Now we just needed a chauffeur. The car was expensive, but hiring a chauffeur was surprisingly affordable, so the hard part was done.

The seller dropped the car off at *Nanu*'s place, expecting I'd take it for a spin, but there was one tiny problem: I didn't know how to drive and Rajesh was doing a piss poor job of teaching me. Naturally, my khalas, knowing how well-connected I was, came to me for help finding a chauffeur. So, I made a call to a guy, my youngest *mama*, who told me about a man who had just arrived in Dhaka from a village in Gaibandha district, got his driver's license, and was looking for work. Now, I'm not about to send my baby sister on a death ride, but I do believe in giving people a fair chance. So, what better way to test his driving skills than by sitting in the front passenger seat with only me as a witness? I may not know how to drive, but I sure know when I'm about to die.

The guy showed up on time, and we went for a drive. While a little rough around the edges, he wasn't half-bad—nothing I couldn't see improving with time. So, we had ourselves a chauffeur, a good looking, pale young man in plain torn clothing named Ranjan Marya. When I went to save his contact on my phone, I realised I already knew someone else named Ranjan. To avoid accidentally messaging the wrong person, I saved this Ranjan's contact as "Driver Mary" because my phone would only let me save up to eleven characters. It quickly became an inside joke among the boys, and soon enough, Shiro and Rajesh started calling him Mary without ever bothering to know his actual name. But despite the teasing, Ranjan seemed like a nice guy.

Ranjan quickly became part of the family. He'd join us for meals and relish whatever Mom or *Nanu* had prepared. Living in a joint family gave us a strong sense of community, and we happily shared that with Ranjan. My mamas and khalas would often drop by, sparking lively conversations that filled the room with laughter and warmth. At first, Ranjan was taken aback by being invited to sit down and eat with us—it was a gesture he said he had never experienced with anyone he'd worked for. But over time, he got used to it and started looking forward to it.

Having the car meant that Mahi, Nessa, and Sammy now had more flexibility when it came to choosing tutors—proximity was no longer an issue. But, of course, Mom being my Mom, became extra cautious about who Sammy interacted with, especially since she was reaching that age where love affairs weren't out of the question. Sammy, being as gullible as she was, had a tendency to pick the wrong people, and Mom wasn't as observant of people as I was, after all!

It was around that time I noticed Sammy was spending more and more time "at the tutor's" after school. My Mom picked up on it too, frequently calling Ranjan, who'd confirm that he was still parked outside her supposed classroom and that he'd seen her go in. After one too many evenings, Mom finally confronted her one afternoon as she was about to leave for class, dressed up as if for a special event.

"Tell me the truth," she asked, his voice calm but pointed, "Do you really have classes this late, every day?"

Sammy was quick to respond, snapped, "Yes, I do. Please just leave me alone!"

We now had separate rooms as Mom rented the small flat next to *Nanu's*. I was eavesdropping from behind my door, sitting on my bed in a T-shirt and shorts, pretending not to listen. There was a pause, and then Mom added, "You look like you're going to a palace to study royalty."

Sammy, unaware of the sarcasm, shot back with a casual, "Thank you!"

"That wasn't a compliment," Mom sneered. "I don't know where you're going, but you're taking Sufi with you—and he's not waiting in the car with Ranjan."

Sammy's voice erupted in disbelief. "What!?" she cried, and without thinking, I too spoke the same "What!?" from behind the door, inadvertently giving myself away.

Within seconds, she stormed into my room, grabbed my arm, and barked, "Let's go, now!" Still half-dressed, I scrambled to grab my phone and wallet from the table, hopping on one foot as I threw on my flip-flops and stumbled after her.

As we headed out the door, Mom shouted, "Sufi! Keep an eye on her!"

In the car, Sammy settled into the back seat while I occupied the front passenger seat and Ranjan took the wheel. It felt like just another ordinary trip to her classes. I remained quiet throughout the journey, sensing Sammy's growing annoyance. As we approached the building, we got out as Ranjan took the car away to park.

We walked into the building, and I finally broke the silence, asking, "Are you taking me inside too? Or should I wait somewhere here?"

"Shush! I'm just waiting for Ranjan to drive around the corner so he can't see us leave!" she whispered fiercely.

I couldn't help but smile. "I knew there was more to it."

"Shut up and follow me!" she snapped just as our car turned the corner. Then, in a surprising burst of energy, she sprinted across the street in her heels while I trailed behind in flip-flops, wondering how she maintained her balance in those shoes. Sure, she could roller skate when she was younger, but heels were a different story!

On the other side of the street, she dashed towards a car with tinted windows. "Get in the back and please don't ruin this for me!" she urged, almost out of breath. Confused and slightly scared, I climbed into the unfamiliar ride without question.

As I settled into the back seat, I watched through the tinted glass as Sammy paused before the front passenger door, took a deep breath, and adjusted her clothes and left eye patch. Then, almost trying too hard to appear elegant, she opened the door and slid into the seat. I turned my gaze from her to the driver's seat, where a boy about our age, dressed in a formal shirt and dress pants, stared back at me, his mouth partially open in disbelief.

He quickly turned to Sammy, his expression shifting from shock to irritation. "I asked YOU out on a date! Who is that?" he pointed at me, bewildered.

"That's my brother. We're twins. I couldn't leave without taking him with me," she replied nonchalantly.

He composed himself and extended his hand towards the back seat in an attempt to shake mine, introducing himself with a forced smile. I obliged, not bothering to remember his name, knowing Sammy wouldn't date him for long anyway if my bat had anything to say about it!

We drove passed Ranjan who was standing outside the car about to light a cigarette., Sammy broke the silence, asking, "So, are we going to the bridge?"

I leaned forward, alarm bells blaring in my mind. "What bridge?" I asked, keeping my voice steady in an attempt to mask the edge creeping into my tone.

The boy, glancing at me with a grin, said, "I planned to take Sammy to Padma Bridge to watch the sunset and enjoy dinner—I have some snacks in the back. What couples usually do on a first date!"

I glanced beside me and noticed a small bag filled with sandwiches and drinks, just enough for two. My mind raced with questions. "But Padma Bridge is almost 50 kilometres away! How are we supposed to drive up there and be back before your classes start?"

Sammy rolled her eyes. "First, I don't have classes today, and second, we'll be a little late...for dinner"

"Sure," I muttered, feeling a bead of sweat form as worry gnawed at me about not returning on time and raising a red flag with Mom!

I decided to quiet my concerns, giving them the chance to enjoy this awkward drive. The boy skilfully navigated the stick shift, his left hand constantly hovering over the transmission gear. Sister dearest attempted to be romantic, resting her hand over his a few times, only to be met with the awkward realisation that her older brother was sitting in the back, wearing flip-flops and shorts, judgmentally observing them while the boy fidgeted in discomfort.

Despite the initial tension, we eventually reached Padma Bridge. To my surprise, the boy and I found some common ground, and by the end of the evening, all three of us were having a good time. As night fell, he dropped us off a street away from Sammy's classes, aware that Ranjan would be standing in front of the building, and Sammy preferred not to be caught.

We got out, and Sammy snuck up to Ranjan and playfully tapped on his shoulder, declaring, "Ranjan bhai, let's go! I'm done!" Ranjan was not surprised at all, as if he had seen her do this countless times before.

But of course, Sammy and happy endings just don't seem to go hand in hand. I had been really rooting for her with this guy—he seemed like a good one. So, when I casually asked her the following week about their next date, hoping to tag along as the unofficial chaperone again, she dropped the bomb. The boy had called her a "cyclops" to his friends at school and revealed that it was all part of a "social experiment turned prank." Apparently, he had an entire camera setup in his car, planning to record an internet video titled *"My Date with a Cyclops."*

I must have foiled his plan by being there the first time. But the damage was already done. This is why I can't stand pranksters who call their antics "social experiments." Degenerate lowlifes, the lot of them—playing with someone's emotions for likes and shares. Naturally, Sammy became even more distant with any boy who tried to approach her afterward. Who could blame her?

I wasn't about to let that little sh*t get away with what he'd done to my sister. Sitting on *Nanu*'s porch, I vented my anger to Rajesh. I saw a glint in his eyes as he leaned forward and said, "I have an idea."

So, guess what? I pulled a prank on the prankster. Let's just say there's now a video floating around online where he's running across the Padma Bridge, stark naked, screaming, *"It's just a prank, bro!"* And yes, he stripped down willingly—though it didn't take *too* much persuasion. Turns out, Rajesh had this uncanny ability to stand someone down with just a look, like a village elder delivering silent judgment. Good guy to have around in a pinch.

Now, Diary, I'm not a loveless weirdo, although most of my conversations have been with my boys on MSN messenger. When I skipped a year, I thought about plenty of things that I could do as a business hustle.

Dhaka was experiencing a street food and fast food revolution. Junk food stalls were popping up on every corner, similar to the wave that once hit America and pushed it toward an obesity crisis—ah, progress! It was thanks to some very astute individuals who realised the need for accessible food options for students and office workers, leading to the rise of both roadside vendors and franchise giants. Entrepreneurs saw opportunity, and soon there were two clear camps in the junk food industry.

On one hand, you had the hard-working swindlers, selling god-knows-what, often crow meat disguised as chicken, at prices cheaper than chicken feed. On the other hand, there were enterprising rich kids, using family money to open flashy stalls, hiring someone to run things while they occasionally showed up to collect the profits—and got upset when they realised success actually required effort.

For established businessmen, the obvious choices were eateries, pharmacies, or hospitals. The logic was simple: you eat until you feel queasy, then you buy medicine, and if things get worse, you check into a hospital. The picture of progress, right?

I also noted that this extended to beauty products with beauty salons now taking over. We're catching up with the Western obsession over beauty products, where anyone who can spell "conditioner" claims to be a beauty expert. They peddle products to young women already made insecure by decades of "Fair & Lovely" ads that glorified lighter skin and mocked darker tones. The irony, of course, is that women in the West spend big money to get the very skin tone these ads once disparaged. Funny how things come full circle.

So, I took both ideas and combined them together to create a disaster of a business pitch, a cart that sells samosas and a local brand of shaving cream! That was an epic disaster, but I still had one regular customer. Tanya, A lively bubbly girl definitely much smarter than I will ever be. She was also taller than me which I really liked! Diary, I did not have a fetish, just letting you know! Tanya did however have an absolutely terrible taste in friends—myself very much included.

Suddenly, I had another person to chat with on MSN Messenger, and she was always kind to me. We spoke almost every other night, but

I never found the courage to confess my feelings. I often tried to compliment her in my own clumsy attempts at flirting, but I never knew how to follow through. This inevitably led to prolonged, awkward silences, where she would graciously step in and change the subject, saving us both from the discomfort I'd created. One day on MSN messenger, instead of changing the topic, she outright messaged me if I liked her. In a fit of panic, I jumped up, ran around my room to let off steam, gathered my composure, imagined what our life together might look like, and finally returned to the keyboard to type 'no.'

I stared at my response in disbelief, wide-eyed and hands on my head, until she replied with a simple 'okay.' In hindsight, high school relationships rarely last beyond the first prom, and even for that brief moment, she dodged a bullet!

Now, I want to clarify that this isn't a cliché story about a romantic reunion or rekindling lost love. She moved on and is dating someone who owned a Toyota Camry! But it was me who pulled away from her, not the other way around. The reason? She had a "whale" of a friend—probably tipping the scales at 1000 kilos (exaggerated!) crammed into a 153 cm frame. Now, before you call me a bigot for fat-shaming, hear me out: this wasn't about body positivity. I've met plenty of lovely overweight people who understood their bodies and made an effort to accommodate those around them—but she was definitely not one of them! She was fat and rude by *choice*.

Even after Tanya introduced me to her as "just a friend," she actually said, "You have to be six feet tall for me to consider you boyfriend material!" To which I, with unparalleled grace, replied, "Says the girl who is six feet wide!" She called me narrow-minded and accused me of fat-shaming her!

My samosa business? Gone. She ate half my profits and never paid a damn penny for it, then had the audacity to call me cheap when I asked her to pay up! And don't think for a second she had an ounce of self-awareness. When Tanya herself gently suggested skipping the extra cheese on her triple-cheese burger, she puffed up with righteous indignation. There's being overweight because of some metabolic disorder beyond your control, and then there's *this whale*—justifying her morbid obesity as something society should not only accept but celebrate. All the while, no one can even share a rickshaw ride with her without clinging to the edge for dear life, dodging death as cars in the other lane grazed their bum, dangling precariously off the side. Yet she still expected to split the fare like it's some kind of fair partnership! Obesity is not healthy! It has cardiovascular health risks for both her *and* the person sharing a rickshaw ride with her!

Oh, but it doesn't stop there. The "whale" had this brilliant idea to try vodka and weed, and who does Tanya ask to acquire it? Me, of course. She chugged the vodka like it was water, passed out, and left *us* to deal with the fallout. Poor Rajesh still complains about his back after hauling her blubbery body downstairs that night. Then she had the gall to tell Tanya that Rajesh groped her which Tanya believed! Tanya wouldn't believe me when I told her the whale was hallucinating and doing it to herself! I had enough.

Sammy encouraged me to keep putting myself out there and even suggested online dating sites that did not claim there were hundreds of desperate white housewives waiting for me in Oldtown, Dhaka. Who would've thought that in the modern world, you could pick potential dates by swiping through profiles like trading Pokémon cards? Intrigued but clueless, I decided to give it a shot.

Of course, being a rookie, I made the classic mistake of uploading my first profile picture with the boys. I sent Shiro a screenshot of it on MSN. Shiro replied back to me with a virtual facepalm emoji. "Bro," he said, "you need to look seductive! Show some abs and crop Rajesh out!"

Suffice to say, my experiences with online dating were... well, mixed. My match count was an impressive one! That's right—just one.

That one match haunted me for a while. It's hard to take anyone seriously online when they lie about their name, age, height, occupation, preferences, gender, and even personality. So, when my match told me she was a Bangladeshi-American studying medicine, visiting Bangladesh on holiday, I was sceptical but thought I'd be lucky if the only person I matched with wasn't a middle-aged bald guy operating out of his basement looking to catfish me, knock me out, and sell my kidneys on eBay. She asked to meet, and I agreed. To my surprise, she looked exactly like her profile picture. How about that?

However, things quickly took a turn for the worse after we met. I can't recall the exact conversation, but she was unsettling to be around. I decided to be polite and finish the meal, but when I told her I'd like to leave, she asked me to show her where I lived. Mind you, this was quite recent, and I had already overcome many of the insecurities I faced as a child. I thanked her for the offer but insisted I'd be on my way. We hugged, but she didn't seem happy about my decision to leave.

As I hopped onto a rickshaw, I noticed she hailed one behind me. At first, I thought nothing of it, but after traveling a few kilometres, I looked back through the opening in the rickshaw hood and saw her following me! She had claimed to live in the opposite direction, which made me uneasy. I decided to change my route to a random address down the street, and sure enough, she followed me there. When I got off the rickshaw, I saw her rickshaw pass mine as if she were trying to hide that she was on my trail. It felt like a scene from Grand Theft Auto: Rickshaw Edition!

I focused on her rickshaw, which stopped a few buildings down. As she paid her rickshaw puller, I darted across the street and disappeared into the labyrinth of alleyways. For three straight days, I spotted her in front of where I got off that night. We made eye contact, but she never spoke, and I ignored her completely and walked past her. On the third day, I decided to go to the police station to report the situation.

The male officer filing the report sat down with me and asked, "So, describe your 'stalker' to me. How tall is she? What's her build?"

"Likely 155 cm, petite," I replied.

"And how tall are you?" he continued.

"178 cm. Where are you going with this?"

The officer chuckled, "Are you afraid she might overpower you in a dark alleyway, big man?" He laughed and added, "There's nothing to report here. If she wants to stare, let her stare. Just don't stare back—that would be harassment!"

Thankfully, she stopped following me after the fourth day—or if she continued, I never saw her again, which was fine by me!

In the end, Sammy and my younger cousins, Mahi, and Nessa became my pals and fooled around while I finally matured enough to take on the role of the protective brother. Shiro, would often tag along whenever I mentioned spending time with my cousins. At first, I didn't think much of it, but as it became a recurring pattern, I started to get suspicious. I couldn't help but notice how his gaze lingered on Sammy at every gathering, clearly smitten, yet he never said a word. As much as I liked both of them, I wasn't about to play matchmaker for Shiro. I don't want a womaniser like Shiro near my baby sister—although, as long as he wasn't bothering anyone, what was the harm in his presence? Its not like they don't talk at school. Diary, I don't know if a person can change all of their habits for one girl, and I sure as hell won't take that chance with Sammy who has already been through a lot.

We spent time together, with them talking about their latest pranks at school, or movies or Anime they had watched, while I listened and offered advice far beyond my years. They laughed at my attempts to sound wise, but in private, they'd often confide in me. As promised, I kept giving Sammy small tips on how I managed to break free from my social awkwardness, peppering in more stories about my misadventures with Shiro and Rajesh. Of course, Shiro couldn't resist inserting himself into the conversation, often exaggerating his role in the stories in a desperate attempt to impress my cousin. Thankfully, Sammy was oblivious to his not-so-subtle hints. Instead, she would sit there, listening intently, scribbling down notes as if I were revealing some grand secret. It was adorable, watching her treat my absurd tales like they were little nuggets of wisdom, when really, I was just trying to make her laugh and help her feel more confident.

I spent my weekend afternoons taking Sammy to the local park gardens, where she loved chasing after ducks like a child. She'd carry her trusty backpack, always packed with a plant encyclopedia she referred to religiously as we strolled past the vibrant array of exotic flora. Though she must have read it dozens of times, I was always amazed by how she could revisit the same pages, marvelling at the plants with genuine awe each time.

"Biology is so interesting," she'd tell me with sparkling eyes. "I'd like to be a doctor someday! Oh maybe do a PhD!"

And I'd always reply, "We'll make it all happen, Sammy. Don't you worry. I won't let anything get in the way of your dreams!"

Watching her play with the ducks and scribble in her picture book amidst familiar scenery we'd visited countless times felt comforting. But gradually over the last 2 months, her enthusiasm started to fade, her behaviour growing increasingly childlike, almost as though she was going backwards to a younger version of herself. Then, she started pulling away entirely, withdrawing from everyone and started missing school and her tutors.

Mom waved it off, chalking it up to being just a phase of growing up. "She'll bounce back," she'd say. But I knew things Sammy told me that she never told Mom. But Sammy never stopped talking to *me,* no matter how much she was cross with me!

One evening, after driving Mahi and Nessa back from their tutors, Ranjan parked the car, and the girls rushed inside, chirping and laughing like they didn't have a care in the world. I waited for the noise to fade before stepping out and calling Ranjan over for a private chat.

"Ranjan, have you noticed anything strange about Sammy lately?" I asked, keeping my tone casual.

Ranjan frowned, looking genuinely puzzled. "No, Sufi. She seems fine. Though to be honest, I usually chat with the other drivers while waiting in the parking lot, so I've got no clue what happens during her classes."

I nodded, but I wasn't convinced. "She's not been herself lately," I pressed, hoping he'd remember something.

Ranjan hesitated. "Look, I have a little sister too, and I can tell if something isn't fine. Sammy goes in on time, comes out on time—nothing seems out of the ordinary."

I gave Ranjan a pat on the back. Good man, I thought, but maybe he was missing something. With no new leads, I decided to call Shiro.

"Bruv," I began, cutting straight to the point. "Have you or Rajesh noticed anything strange with Sammy lately?"

Shiro sounded confused. "No, man. Since we flunked and are repeating a year, and she's technically a senior, we don't cross paths much. Why? What's up?"

"Something isn't adding up. She's not herself at all," I said, sort of frustrated by now.

Shiro was never one to miss an opportunity, "Does she need some company?"

"Not yours, I assure you," I shot back before hanging up.

With no answers and a growing sense of unease, I turned to self-help videos and online guides. I replaced movie time with "Guides to Effective Communication 101," and my late nights were spent scrolling through articles on mental health and spotting signs of distress. I figured if I couldn't get answers from anyone else, I'd damn well learn to ask the right questions myself.

Last week, *that* day came—a day I still wish I could wake up from like a bad dream. Rajesh shared a video in my social media inbox. It had no thumbnails, just a black screen, so I clicked it. The footage was shaky, like one of those old home videos, and it focused on a dingy, dimly lit room. The sound of a drill whined in the background.

Once the camera steadied, I saw an overweight man holding a tattooing drill, etching something on the chest of a petite girl. She was squirming, biting her lip, and doing her best to cover the exposed part of her chest with her opposite hand. My stomach dropped—f*ck, Sammy was getting a tattoo.

The girl filming it chuckled softly and whispered commentary into the mic. "I can't believe she's actually doing it," she mocked Sammy. It hit me like a slap—I knew that voice. Ayesha. That smug b*tch who had been picking on Sammy at school for years. "She just doesn't get sarcasm!" she added with a giggle.

Another voice chimed in, a guy's voice. "Look at her trying to hide her non-existent t*ts! You think Cyclops'll do me if we tell her that's the only way to get the bullying to stop?"

Before I could even process the rage bubbling inside me, Rajesh sent another message. "It started circulating today, but this happened last week. Shiro got the video from one of Sammy's classmates."

I felt sick. Sammy had stopped faking classes after the date-gone-wrong fiasco—or so I thought. I decided it was time to confront her, but this time, I'd use all the "effective communication" techniques I'd been studying.

I walked into her room knowing she came back home early from school and sat down on the edge of her bed. She was lying on her side, her back to me.

"Sammy," I started gently, "you saw the video, didn't you?"

Without turning around, she sighed. "Yeah. You saw it too?"

"I did," I replied. "Mind telling me what that was all about?"

She turned slightly, just enough for me to see her face. "They kept calling me a sl*t, saying I'd blow anyone if the price was right. I thought if I didn't react, the rumours would die down. But Ayesha controlled the narrative. She made sure everyone believed her."

"People gossip all the time, Sammy," I said, trying to reassure her. "Doesn't mean it's true."

Her eyes filled with tears. "I'm related to you. And they say you were Frankie's coke dealer, that you sold her bad stuff, and she took it out on my eye. They say your 'goons' spend their nights taking turns on me."

That felt like a punch to my guts. "Sammy, I know you. None of that is true!"

Sammy let out a heavy sigh. "I begged Ayesha to stop, to cut it out with the lies. I told her how hurtful it was, but she just smirked and said, 'Fine. Get a tattoo, and we'll stop.'"

She paused, looking up to the ceiling. "I told her, 'I don't know any tattoo artists.' And she just grinned and said, 'Oh, we can arrange that.'"

Sammy glanced up at me, "And I said... 'okay, done.'"

She sighed again and slowly pulled down the neckline of her T-shirt, just enough to reveal the tattoo under her collarbone. My jaw dropped. I couldn't even tell what it was supposed to be from this angle, but to me, it looked disturbingly like a badly drawn sperm. The skin around it was red, swollen, and oozing— it was infected.

I told her, "Sammy a doctor needs to see this, the skin is infected" to which she simply nodded and continued with her confession.

"I thought if I went through with it, they'd stop," she said quietly.

The guys filming in the room told Ayesha to make me do the tattoo over my left breast so that I couldn't see what they were marking on me.

I clenched my fists, trying to suppress the anger boiling inside me. "Sammy, it's *illegal* for minors to get tattoos. And even if it wasn't—do you honestly think they would've stopped?"

She looked away. "But Ayesha said they would."

I shook my head. "Everybody lies, Sammy. We only tell the truth when it's convenient for us."

Sammy tried to muster a weak smile but it quickly faded. "You're right. But now, there's a new rumour—that I'm a 'cum sl*t' who got it tattooed. Sufi, I don't even know what that means! This morning, a bunch of guys came to my desk and threw a milkshake in my face. Then, I was called to the principal's office and got scolded for breaking the school's code of conduct because of the tattoo."

Her voice cracked as she finished, and I stood there, fists clenched, not knowing what to say. "I'm going to have a word with Ayesha," I said finally, the anger simmering under my voice.

Sammy shook her head. "Don't bother. Her parents are shipping her off to Canada next month. Anything you do in the meantime will just make it worse for me."

And she wasn't wrong. Rich kids like Ayesha got to wreak havoc on others, then pack up and disappear to start fresh in the West, leaving the mess behind. Not everyone who migrates is like that, sure, but there are criminals who deserve to be dragged back and held accountable for the damage they've caused in Bangladesh.

I sighed, standing up from the bed. "Fine. Violence won't solve anything here. But I need to talk to the boys. I think you should tell Mom. Maybe there's something else we can do."

Sammy sounded defeated as she turned over, pulling the blanket up to her chin. "Fine. I'll tell her when I'm ready. Right now I'm going to take a nap."

"Alright. We'll talk when you wake up."

I left her room and headed to the porch, where Ranjan was waiting with a cigarette already lit. We sat in silence for a moment before I started talking. "I don't know what the f*ck to do, Ranjan. Violence just escalates things—it's like playing with fire. But if I don't do something, Sammy's going to keep getting hurt."

Ranjan exhaled a cloud of smoke, nodding thoughtfully, but for once, he didn't have any clever ideas. We sat there scheming as the sun began to dip below the horizon, but nothing seemed like a real solution. I had to be strategic.

When dusk came, Ranjan handed me the car keys and got up to leave. "I've got to pick up my sister from somewhere," he said.

"Good on you," I muttered, watching him disappear into the night. At least he was looking out for his sister—something I was beginning to feel like I'd failed to do for mine.

That evening, I gave Mom a heads-up about the conversation she'd likely need to have with Sammy later. Mom, being Mom, rolled her eyes and called me an idiot for assuming she wouldn't know how to handle her own daughter.

"Go get your sister. Let's have dinner first," she said.

I nodded and headed to Sammy's room. When I got there, the door was locked. I knocked. "Sammy, dinner time!"

No response.

I knocked again, louder this time. "Sammy, come on! Don't make me drag you out."

Still nothing.

Frustration started bubbling up. I banged on the door harder. "I know you're upset, Sammy but please open the damn door!"

When there was still no response, I sighed and went back to Mom. "She's not answering. Can you grab the spare key? I'm not playing this 'go away, I'm not hungry' game tonight."

Mom shot me a concerned look but didn't say anything. She rummaged through a drawer and handed me the key.

I wish she'd just yelled at me instead. I wish Sammy had yelled back through the door, told me to leave her alone. I wish for anything but what came next.

I unlocked the door and pushed it open.

Mom's scream pierced through the house, and my knees buckled.

There she was. My baby sister, hanging from the ceiling fan, her lifeless body swaying gently in the dark room.

"Sammy..." I whispered, hoping either she'd respond, or I'd wake myself up. But it didn't matter. Nothing mattered anymore.

Sufi | Entry 4. Different lives

DIARY,

...

It has been a year since my last confession and oh boy I have a lot to write about. We all took Sammy's passing hard. Even in death, she couldn't escape the cruelty. The self-proclaimed pious elders decided she couldn't be buried in the conventional graveyard because, according to them, she'd died a "dishonourable" death. I wanted to fight them—wanted to grab my bat and remind them what dishonourable actually looked like—but Sammy had always taught me that being diplomatic was better. So, for her sake, I swallowed my rage and kept my fists in my pockets.

Shame, though. Sammy's buried so far away now, in a place called Naria that's hard to visit regularly. Mahi and Nessa say it's for the best, that it'll help me move on. They're probably right. If she were close by, I'd spend every waking moment at her grave, stuck in the past.

Sammy had dreams, big ones. She wanted to study biology, become a doctor, and maybe even do a PhD. I don't know if I'm smart enough to pull it off, but I've decided to try in her honour. It's the least I can do for her. If it were up to the school, they'd have never let me in, but the court mandate left them no choice.

The whole thing was part of a settlement for our property estate. The terms stated that one of the twins had to go back to school—otherwise, Aunt Jenny would've unleashed her legal hellfire on us again. So, I rejoined school after almost two years away.

They put me in year nine, even though I was old enough to be my classmates' dad. I was almost three years older than everyone in my class, and they made sure I felt it. They avoided me, whispering behind my back, calling me names like "delinquent," "psycho," and the classic "troublemaker."

Not that it mattered. Rajesh and Shiro, my supposed mates, were no better. They were in year ten and still mocked me for being stuck in year nine. As if they had room to talk—those idiots failed twice themselves.

During recess, I sat with the two idiots, Ranjan and Rajesh, who were huddled over a piece of paper like they were planning a bank heist. What caught my eye were the words *"anal"* and *"foot"* scrawled in bold, underlined twice. Naturally, I leaned in and asked, "What the hell are you writing, Rajesh?"

Rajesh fumbled with the paper like I'd caught him smuggling state secrets. "It's... uh... nothing. Just... you know how some content online is behind paywalls? And you wouldn't want to use a credit card because, uh, reasons?"

"Oh, totally. Reputation," I said, barely holding back a laugh.

"Well," Rajesh continued, "there's this guy who can bypass the wall and get it for you."

Now I was intrigued. "Sounds like a guy worth knowing! What does he charge?"

Shiro decided to chime in. "Charge? Rajesh is a cheap ass. He wouldn't pay a dime even if his life depended on it. The Porno King does this for free."

I nearly spat out my drink. "*Porno King?* What in the shady underworld nonsense is going on here?"

Shiro replied, "He's legit. Total pro. You give him a slip of paper with what you want, along with an empty thumb drive, and he delivers the goods. Sometimes, he even does *home delivery.*"

By this point, I was in tears laughing. "No way. And he does this *for free?* What's his angle? Is he mining crypto from your weird porn requests? What's he getting out of it?"

Rajesh crumpled the paper and threw it into the bin, looking more annoyed than embarrassed. "How about you go ask him yourself, Sherlock? Genius idea, right?"

"Brilliant," I said, grinning. "Point me to this altruistic sm*t dealer, and I'll get to the bottom of it."

At lunch, the boys pointed him out—a scrawny, awkward kid at least 3 to 4 years younger than me, sitting alone, eating a sandwich like it was his only friend in the world. He didn't exactly scream *kingpin,* more like a guy who would devote all their life to playing Dungeons and Dragons.

Yet, something about him made me feel bad. Maybe it was the loneliness, or maybe it was the idea that this kid, dubbed the *Porno King,* was providing this bizarre public service without anyone bothering to ask if *he* was okay.

"I'm gonna talk to him," I said to Rajesh and Shiro.

They smirked. "Good luck, hero! But word is, he doesn't talk to anyone unless it's about porn! So make sure you throw in a request for something, otherwise, he'll just sit there like a mute freak!"

I shot back, "Yeah, and there were rumours about Sammy too. Didn't make them true!"

Rajesh quickly chimed in, "Come on, man, don't drag Sammy into this. I'll never be able to jerk off thinking about that!" He glanced at Shiro for support.

Shiro stayed quiet.

Rajesh ran back to the trash bin, fished out the crumpled paper, and handed it to me. "That's fine, but keep this just in case. If the porno king asks, tell him you want this!"

I groaned, "I'm not going to request something for you!"

Rajesh gave me those sad puppy dog eyes, so I relented. When I read what he had written, I almost threw up. I felt like dipping my eyes in holy water just to cleanse myself. If I had to write that down, I'd burn this entire diary. Hell, I could barely talk to the porno king as it was, let alone after Rajesh put that image in my head!

I walked up to him, but I could feel eyes boring into my back as I did. The last thing I wanted was to make his life harder at school by being seen talking to me. So, I did what any genius in a bind would do—I lied. "Hey, we're playing football at the community field. "You should join us," I said casually. A little white lie wouldn't hurt, right?

I had this gut feeling about him, like I already knew what might be running through his head. The open field seemed like a safer bet—less claustrophobic, more neutral. I figured he'd feel more comfortable there. Sammy would've liked it too.

And that's how I met Yaad. He turned out to be the smartest person I've ever met, but just as naïve about the world as Sammy was. It blew my mind when I found out why he was giving away porn like some X-rated Robin Hood. The guy wasn't doing it for laughs or thrills—he just wanted to interact with people. The poor bast*rd thought slinging sm*t would buy him some social currency.

He needed to see the world, learn how to stand his ground, so he wouldn't keep getting taken advantage of. And sure, I wasn't exactly a saint swooping in to save him. I had my reasons too. Yaad was a solid student—freakishly good, actually—and if I was serious about becoming a doctor and doing a PhD someday, I needed tutoring. Mom was already stretched thin financially, so paying for extra help was out of the question.

Despite excelling in all the subjects that truly mattered, Yaad was constantly criticised by a few schoolteachers for his less-than-perfect English speaking and writing skills. The hypocrisy was in the fact that it was always the local brown teachers—those with their international degrees and self-proclaimed cosmopolitan flair. They would go out of their way to berate a brown fellow like Yaad for being "inarticulate," while simultaneously praising our only French exchange student, whose English was far worse, as "trying their best since English isn't their first language." Never once did I see a native English speaker comment on Yaad's linguistic shortcomings. It was always our own people, trapped in a post-colonial inferiority complex, desperate to prove their superiority by tearing down one of their own.

Yaad agreed to help me out. And honestly? Even if he'd said no, I would've still wanted to be his friend. The kid wasn't half bad. A little weird, sure, but in a good way.

The first thing he said to me during our first tutoring session was, "You swear and curse way too much," and, annoyingly, he sounded sincere. According to him, I could get my point across just fine without peppering it with profanities. Though I resisted at the time, when I reflected on it later, I knew he wasn't wrong. Most people around me growing up swore pointlessly because they thought it made them seem cool, and naturally, I copied them like an overexcited parrot without realising that it makes people look like uneducated wannabes.

Even though the guy barely knew me, he made me promise to quit swearing and cursing. For reasons even I can't explain, I actually agreed. Maybe I was caught off guard, or maybe I just didn't want to crush his optimism—The kid started looking up to me. Either way, here I am, attempting to turn over a new leaf and keep my story clean, starting...now!

The boys and I started spending more time with Yaad. He mentioned that his dad was strict and kept a tight leash on him, enforcing curfews that made it impossible to do anything after 8:00 pm. So, we planned all our activities during the day to squeeze as much out of the time as we could. This meant he'd tutor me after school, and then we'd head off to play football. The kid was practically growing up glued to a screen, and the only muscles he was probably developing were the ones in his left arm. The boys and I would occasionally abduct him when his dad was away on business trips, whisking him away on all-night road trips—courtesy of Rajesh!

With the long commute from Oldtown to Uttara, I'd sometimes crash at Rajesh's four-story mansion—seriously, I still have no clue what his parents do for a living to afford all that; Every time I asked him, he gave me bizarre answers. I got us all enrolled into the local football youth club. We met some interesting people at the field, but a few stood out: Ryan, Zahin, and then there was Amjad, the self-proclaimed son of a billionaire and Ayesha's sister. Yes, the same Ayesha who, in my mind, was the one who pushed Sammy over the edge.

Diary, if you're thinking getting Yaad to play football was just a random excuse to get closer to Amjad, you're partially right. Even after a year, I still couldn't shake the feeling that there was something unresolved in me about Sammy's situation. I can't afford a trip to Canada to confront Ayesha, but getting to know Amjad could give me some closure—maybe he wasn't as much of a piece of work as his older sister. Naturally, he didn't recognise me, but how could he? Sammy probably didn't matter to him, and even if Ayesha mentioned it, I bet they were rich enough to simply forget.

In the beginning, we just played football without much talking. Shiro and Rajesh were utterly useless at the sport, and Yaad could barely manage a proper kick. Honestly, the only thing I was good at involved swinging cricket bats at...things. When we were struggling to even look like a team, a local kid named Ryan came over and offered to teach us a few things. He was a lanky kid who disclosed to everyone that he was queer in a way that did not seem like he was seeking attention or validation—as it should be. Ryan was genuinely nice and I was just glad someone was helping Yaad out. And to my surprise, Yaad picked up football faster than I expected.

In a few days, our ragtag group caught the attention of a middle-aged European man. He introduced himself as a professional kids' coach and offered to train us. Yaad and Ryan were all in, thinking it was a great opportunity, but I've been around enough to recognise a swindler, even if I couldn't figure out his angle yet. I managed to tactfully keep Yaad and the boys away from the guy, but Ryan was stubborn and ignored all my hints. He was clearly enamoured with the man, which might have been sweet if it weren't for the fact that the guy was blatantly grooming him! After several failed attempts to talk Ryan out of it, he eventually snapped and told us to leave him alone while they spoke. Trusting my instincts, I decided to involve the others at the field to help drive the guy away from Ryan.

As expected, that didn't sit well with Ryan. He alienated us completely and started meeting the European in private on the side of the field. Ryan stopped talking to us altogether. A few days later, I watched in dismay as Ryan shook hands with the European, walked away with him, and got into his car. It seemed Ryan had finally agreed to "coaching" sessions at the man's personal indoor training deck.

Some of the other kids on the field started making inappropriate jokes about Ryan's sexuality, suggesting he was enjoying the European's attention way too much because it was exotic. It might've been true, but it was still uncool—and Ryan was a minor, for God's sake. My gut was telling me something wasn't right, and I wish I had acted sooner. A day later, Ryan was declared missing. A week later, they found him on the other side of the city. floating face-down in a lake—pants missing, his body showing signs of sexual assault.

The European man? The evidence against him was weak, no DNA tests were conducted, and Ryan's parents couldn't afford to hire a lawyer to press charges. In the end, the man was handed over to his embassy, which promptly advised him to leave Bangladesh before things escalated further. And just like that—no charges, no trial, nothing.

When the news broke, the boys and I attended Ryan's janazah, our equivalent of a funeral prayer. Yaad was absolutely heartbroken for his friend. Diary, people often think we don't welcome other religions at our gatherings, but that's not true. Shiro and Rajesh were just as welcome at Ryan's janazah as anyone else. Although, I wished Zahin hadn't been. As we stood there, Zahin joined us. He sneered and said something I'll never forget:

"Ryan probably died having too much fun. We shouldn't even be hosting a janazah for this."

Yaad didn't hold back. "You wouldn't be saying that if the deceased were your loved one," he shot back.

But Zahin, in his arrogance, doubled down. "Some people just aren't important, Yaad. Last year, I ran over a construction worker. I was drunk, had no license, and ended up with a man under my car. The police showed up and escorted me home. No one remembers that worker; there were no charges because my life was more important. Celebrities coming out as gay? Now that's news—you can spin it into a trend, make money off it, and influence people like Ryan to follow. But Ryan? He was gay *and* poor. His life doesn't matter. People will forget him in no time. He's just a nobody."

It boiled my blood. Rajesh had to hold Shiro back from decking Zahin right there. His mentality reeked of privilege; the kind bred by certain rich parents who preach tradition while shielding their kids' recklessness from justice. They fight tooth and nail against change but have no problem shipping their spoiled brats overseas for "multicultural education," probably funded by ill-gotten gains stolen from the very "nobodies" they look down on. Hypocrites, the lot of them.

But thankfully Zahin wouldn't ever get that chance. A couple of months later, he crashed his car on the Dhaka-Sylhet highway near the grand junction while drunk. Apparently, another driver pressured him into speeding, and he lost control, skidding off to avoid a collision. His car got obliterated by an oncoming bus. I know a guy who was there who said Zahin died gasping for air, suffocating against the airbag while no one bothered to help.

Yaad was right: karma really is a b*tch.

I had to make sure no one came after *our* anuses, so I enrolled the lot into Karate. Yaad claimed he knew Taekwondo, but the kid couldn't even defend himself when Shiro smacked him in the head a few times. He started crying, and Shiro ended up apologising! Sigh...Yaad.

Our karate journey didn't last long, though—not because I got so good I challenged my instructor and beat him. Yeah, that didn't happen. Turned out, our instructor was a peeping tom who fell off a tree while on "duty" outside a girls' dormitory. He broke his legs *and* his penis.

We stuck to football for the time being as I gradually got closer to Amjad, bit by bit. Amjad wasn't as bad as I expected. Sure, he had a knack for showing off, constantly bragging about how every girl under the sun was apparently swooning over him. And then there was his odd habit of conveniently only having 100 takas on him for lunch, despite being the self-proclaimed son of a billionaire. Naturally, he'd order food well beyond 100 takas and ask the rest of us to cover the difference. I guess that's how you stay a billionaire—off the blood, sweat, and tears of others!

One day, Amjad approached me and asked, "So, are the rumours true?"

I responded with a measured calmness, "Believing rumours is a dangerous habit, Amjad. Now, what exactly do you want?"

Amjad smirked and said, "I have a friend who knows Tanya. She said you can get booze and pot easily! Think you can hook me up?"

It was a small world indeed. As much as I disliked the idea, I recognised this as a good opportunity to gain Amjad's trust. Alcohol was harder to come by than escorts in this strange country, but I had a friend who owed me a favour and occasionally supplied me with bottles. I played it cool and asked, "What kind of liquor are you after?"

Amjad shook his head and clarified, "No, bro. If it were just one bottle, I could've taken it from our hotel bar. I'm thinking much bigger."

I raised an eyebrow, "Hotel bar?"

He nodded nonchalantly. "Yeah, man, my family owns the Padmashetu Hotel. But that's beside the point. I've got a plan to host the biggest underground party in the city—open bar, weed, and everything else you can imagine. But I can't just go about letting anyone in on it!"

I immediately shut it down. "Of course you can't. Because it's illegal, and I'm not helping you."

Amjad leaned in, desperate. "Look, man, pretty please. Ayesha says it's a great way to market a new party pill she came across in Cambodia. If it works, we could start supplying it to hotel guests and beyond."

That name caught my attention. "Ayesha's involved in this?"

"Of course," Amjad said, almost proudly. "It was her idea. She'll be here to bring the goods and hype the market before heading back to Canada. She was touring Asia during her semester breaks when she hit gold!"

I was curious. "And she's carrying contraband through immigration? Won't she get caught?"

Amjad laughed as if I was naive. "Why would she? Everyone knows who Dad is. And besides, she's a girl—Bangladesh customs isn't too strict with women."

I hated the idea, but something instinctively made me agree. "Okay, fine. But this needs to be discreet."

Amjad lit up, practically buzzing with excitement. "Thanks, man, I owe you big time!"

I quickly laid down my terms. "One condition—no minors at the party. How are you sending out invitations, and how will you make sure no kids show up?"

It was clear Amjad hadn't thought any of this through. He asked for my help, and we had a lot of work to do.

First, the venue. Amjad assured me that was covered. Next, the alcohol. We needed a significant amount, and I wasn't sure my contact would entertain such a large request. To my surprise, he agreed, provided the entire payment for a truckload was made upfront. I brought Amjad along to handle that—I wasn't about to invest a single cent.

For the weed, I reached out to Ranjan, who knew some suppliers. That part was sorted quickly.

The real challenge was ensuring discretion. Advertising openly was out of the question—I wasn't about to get myself into trouble. No hard-copy tickets and only anonymous communication. I needed someone skilled with computers, which ruled me out entirely.

As much as I did not want to, I turned to Yaad. I promised myself I'd keep him out of harm's way, framing this as a lesson in what *not* to do at a party—if done under careful supervision.

Within a few days, the invitations had gone out across the city via the dark web, and Yaad knew exactly what he was doing. Soon enough, it was party time. Amjad secured a venue in the poshest area of the city, with a casual dress code to avoid raising suspicion. I showed up with the boys in my usual worn jeans and sandals. I gave Yaad strict instructions to stick with either me or Shiro and Rajesh at all times and not to accept anything anyone offered. We arrived later than planned, as I didn't want Amjad delegating the gatekeeping to us. A guard at the entrance scanned our online tickets with a barcode scanner. Yaad had nailed the ticketing system.

We stepped into the dark, club-like atmosphere—flickering lights, dry ice smoke, people running around with plastic cups in their hands, and the unmistakable smell of beer and sweat. Yaad clung to me from behind, looking more nervous by the second. Maybe this wasn't such a great idea after all.

We made our way to the bar where Amjad spotted us and quickly approached to tell us that Ayesha was impressed by the turnout. He led us over to her, where she was deep in conversation with some friends. Shiro and Rajesh opted to stay by the bar; they had no interest in joining the conversation. I told Yaad to stay with them, but he insisted on seeing more of the party, so I relented.

Amjad introduced me to Ayesha, who stepped forward and gave me a hug. She was every bit the fashionista—poised and graceful, with a look that screamed hours of grooming. Ayesha didn't recognise me, but I remembered her well. I decided to keep that little detail to myself.

Ayesha smiled and said, "This is brilliant, thank you. I've got people going around offering 'Ya ba' to our guests and letting them know where to find more."

As she spoke, Amjad handed Yaad a glass and a "Ya ba," as Ayesha called it. Without breaking my gaze from Ayesha, I took the glass and pill from Yaad's hands and said firmly, "This kind of business is dangerous, especially when you involve family."

Ayesha didn't flinch. "You've done something to Amjad," she said. "He can't stop praising you. You have our thanks, and you can take a cut of tonight's profits."

I politely declined, "Thanks, Ayesha, but I was just helping a friend. Isn't that right, Amjad?"

Amjad stammered, "Yes, absolutely. Anything you need, I'm here for you too!"

We sat down and chatted with Ayesha for a while. She came across as an enterprising woman who clearly prioritised money over everything else. She was surrounded by the children of important figures: the son of a high-ranking police officer, Humayun, the daughter of a foreign diplomat, and, most notably, Ibran—the youngest son of a local pharmaceutical tycoon. Yaad and I found ourselves surrounded by these "nepo" kids, each more important than the last. Every time one of them offered Yaad a drink, I would gently move the glass away, reminding them he was too young.

Ayesha chuckled, "You organized an entire underground party but not old enough to drink?"

Amjad and Ayesha took turns teasing Ibran, calling him a "wh*remonger."

Amjad smirked and asked, "So tell me, Ibran, how does the son of a pious leader like Hossein Al-Giri end up as a regular at every brothel in the city?"

Clearly drunk, Ibran slurred, "Father only pretends to be religious to win favour with the community leaders. He doesn't even know how to pray properly. They once asked him to give a sermon, and he rambled on with random unelated nonsense in front of hundreds of people."

Amjad burst into laughter. "Ah, the apple doesn't fall far from the tree!"

Ayesha jolted in mock surprise. "Pervert!"

Humayun laughed, shaking his head. "It's not just Ibran's dad, his mom's got issues too! She beat their eight-year-old maid to death over a ruined carpet and thought it was a good idea to stuff the body in a grocery sack, then take it to a village hospital, hoping to bribe a doctor into declare it a suicide. Bad luck for her, though—she went to a doctor with a moral compass. If my dad hadn't stepped in, Ibran's mom would've been behind bars by now!"

Ibran shot back, "Laugh all you want, Humayun, the only reason you're sitting in this party is because of me. Who do you think funds your dad and the police for all the nice things you have? Certainly not your dad's meagre salary, but the 'donations' my father and his friends make to yours to look after people like mother."

As they lit up a joint, I grabbed Yaad and pulled him away— I'd had enough of their smug gloating over their victories at the expense of the less fortunate and also there was no way I was letting Yaad passively inhale that garbage.

But Diary, Mom always said that it's not just the rich who are to blame rather the systemic issues. Issues like the general lack of literacy and the overwhelming reliance on outdated methods, superstition, old wives' tales, and blind faith, where questioning is penalised, particularly among the lower and middle classes. She says these classes are easily manipulated with misinformation. A few well-crafted social media posts, and they'll turn on anyone—sometimes so emotionally charged that even the most unconvincing misinformation can rally the masses against a common enemy. While in many cases, their anger is justified, most of the masses don't even know what they're rallying against, making it all too easy for the rich to exploit the classes beneath them. After what I witnessed in that group, I find myself inclined to agree with her.

As we walked back to the bar area, I noticed Ayesha's men handing out pills to patrons who were clearly no older than 14 or 15. I had only one condition—no minors—and yet, here they were, kids openly accepting drugs. Frustrated, I left Yaad with Shiro and Rajesh and stormed over to Amjad, who was lounging on a sofa, clearly drunk.

I nudged him from behind and snapped, "Amjad, we were very clear. Why are there minors at this party?"

Amjad, unamused and slurring his words, replied, "You mean Yaad?"

He wasn't wrong—I had brought Yaad here, which made me just as guilty as anyone else. But that was beside the point. I wasn't about to let the situation spiral any further. Sensing my frustration, Amjad made a feeble attempt to justify the presence of kids. "I don't know, man. Word probably got around. You know how kids are—rich, influential brats likely threatened the gatekeeper with their 'nepo-ness,' and the poor guy caved. That's just how things work."

Before I could respond, Humayun, who had been eavesdropping from a nearby sofa, chimed in with a lazy smirk. "Relax, man. Nothing's going to happen, I assure you. Not at such a lovely event Ayesha's throwing for us." His eyes lingered on Ayesha, his drunken gaze dripping with lust.

Ayesha had barely touched her drink and was sober for the entire conversation. She awkwardly smiled, clearly disgusted by Humayun's advances, and got up to leave the area.

"This is getting out of hand," I muttered under my breath as I returned to the bar and told Shiro, "This is madness."

Shiro was blunt and didn't hold back. "You're the one who orchestrated this. You're one to talk."

Rajesh added, "We should get out of here."

I nodded, agreeing with him. "Go. Take Yaad with you. Rajesh, please drop him home. I'll drop by tomorrow."

As they left, Shiro chuckled over his shoulder, "Let us know which prison to bail you out from."

I shot back, "That won't be necessary."

Determined to clean up the mess, I started with the group of drunk kids clutching the green packs of "ya ba" samples. Without explanation, I snagged the pills from their hands. They were too intoxicated to even notice. Walking through the dimly lit venue, I saw people indulging in various vices and made my way over to Humayun, who was still ogling Ayesha from across the room.

Leaning in, I baited him. "I've seen the way you look at Ayesha. I think she looked at you the same way. She's leaving for Canada in a few days—don't you think now's the time to make your move and give her a night she won't ever forget?"

His fragile ego took the bait. "For sure, man! You're right."

"Just one thing," I added. "Alcohol can make things... difficult, if you know what I mean. You don't want to embarrass yourself in front of Ayesha, do you?" I casually placed a green pack of pills in front of him. "Amjad said these work wonders. I wish I had someone to share the night with—might've popped one myself. But hey, a big man like you probably needs more."

As expected, his testosterone-fuelled intoxicated bravado kicked in. Without a second thought, he popped a couple of pills. "I'm plenty big," he bragged.

I smirked. "I can go around saying I have three heads. Doesn't make it true unless people see it."

Alcohol clouding his judgment, he took the challenge literally. In a moment of drunken bravado, he dropped his pants and stood there, bottomless. "You'll have a hard time walking like that," I said with a straight face. "Leave your pants and shoes here so you don't trip. Go claim your prize, tiger."

To my amusement, he stripped completely, flexing imaginary abs, and strutted through the dimly lit floor looking for Ayesha. What he didn't know was that she had left the venue with Amjad long before I had approached him, and he was ogling at someone else.

Men like to feel useful, and the organ between our legs often becomes either a source of confidence or crippling insecurity, depending on our level of maturity. The truth is, size isn't what matters—knowing how to use it does. Unfortunately, pornography has distorted this perception, fuelling a culture where immature young boys obsess over "sword fighting," metaphorically speaking, to flaunt their manhood, hoping it will earn them admiration. In reality, I've yet to witness a situation outside of porn where a healthy woman enthusiastically exclaims, "Wow, bed me right now!" because a random guy at the park flashes his junk at her unsolicited.

Humayun was no exception to this rule. Fuelled by alcohol and his own insecurities, his judgment was thoroughly clouded, rendering him the perfect example of how fragile masculinity often leads to embarrassing decisions.

Once he was out of sight, I scooped up his clothes and dumped them in a bin in the corner. Then, I walked over to the intoxicated Ibran, borrowing his phone under the pretence that mine had died. I used his phone to call the police and reported that the superintendent's son was in danger, providing them with the location of the party. I handed the phone back to Ibran, thanked him, and calmly exited the venue.

I walked a block away and found a spot at a bus stop—far enough not to draw suspicion but close enough to witness the fallout. I called a guy I knew, a tabloid journalist, and tipped him off about a potential scoop. Within fifteen minutes, his news van pulled up, parked strategically outside, waiting for something juicy and exclusive.

Less than an hour later, the police descended on the scene in full force—at least ten squad cars, an absurd overreaction clearly triggered by the mention of the superintendent's son. I stayed put at the bus stop, watching as they shut the event down. Humayun, still stark naked, was hurriedly escorted out by his father, who had come personally to retrieve him, desperately trying to salvage whatever shred of dignity they had left the journalist scrambled for scandalous soundbites.

One by one, cars with diplomatic crests and other marks of influence began to arrive as panicked parents came to collect their intoxicated, drug-addled children. I sat there on the bench, quietly waiting for my bus, feeling a small sense of satisfaction.

Of course, I knew how the press in my country worked—controlled by the politically connected and the financially powerful. A scandal this big would never see the light of day, at least not in any headline or legitimate outlet. Still, it had been amusing to rattle the privileged dimwits, if only for a moment.

What I hadn't anticipated was the extent of the political reach behind them. Diary, the powers that be didn't let it slide. The next day, their goons showed up at my journalist guy's house and massacred him and his entire family in cold blood for even thinking to publish the scoop. And you wonder why no one speaks up. They have families!

In the coming weeks, Yaad started tutoring me as I made the painfully difficult switch to Science, that consisted of Physics, Chemistry, Biology, and Mathematics. I was determined to follow Sammy's dreams, no matter how challenging it got. Mom finally supported my ambitions, though I suspect it was more out of relief that I was no longer beating people up or getting into trouble.

Most of my time was spent at Yaad's place, hitting the books. His sister was lovely, but his dad was... odd, simply put. When I wasn't there, I'd crash at Rajesh's ridiculously massive mansion. Seriously, what do his parents do for a living? They're never home! The suspense is driving me mad because he's still not telling me!

At some point, I started experiencing chest palpitations that progressively became more frequent, and I started waking up drenched in night sweats. I considered myself healthy—I played football regularly with no issues—but these symptoms worried me. One night, as I lay in bed in one of Rajesh's multiple guest rooms, hoping the palpitations would subside, I told myself, "If this doesn't stop, I'll see a doctor." Just then, my phone rang. It was Mom.

She called to share some good news: she had landed her first real job and was on her way to becoming a certified programmer. I was thrilled for her, but her voice lacked excitement.

"You don't sound as happy as I thought you would," I said.

There was a brief pause before she replied, "Your *Nanu* was diagnosed with late-stage cancer last week. She's scheduled for surgery, and we're all very worried."

I was speechless. "Where's the cancer? How bad is it?" I finally asked.

"They said it's thyroid cancer. They're going to remove part of her neck. But because of her age, they're concerned it may have already spread."

I didn't know how to respond, so I stayed silent as my mother wept softly before steering the conversation back to the usual topics. I chose not to mention my own health issues; she didn't need more worry.

We spoke for another fifteen minutes before she hung up. As I put down the phone, I realised I was sweating profusely, despite the ceiling fan spinning at full speed. Not knowing what else to do, I forced myself to sleep, hoping it would get better by morning.

The day after school, while studying at Yaad's, my palpitations and restlessness gotten worse. It escalated to the point where I had to call Ranjan to pick me up from Uttara and take me back home to Oldtown. Repeating the address to him multiple times only seemed to aggravate my condition further. After what felt like an eternity, Ranjan finally arrived and called me downstairs for the pickup.

Ranjan, usually chauffeured Nessa and Mahi given how unsafe public transport or after-dark travel could be, so I would rarely see him.

However, every time we crossed paths, his wardrobe seemed to grow more ridiculous. He'd taken to replacing his regular attire with cheap designer knockoffs that screamed "*fake it till you make it*".

As soon as I got in the car, his first question wasn't about my condition but, "Whose house is this? I was expecting to pick you up from Rajesh's." Can you believe it? Here I was, clutching my chest like a dying poet, and Ranjan wanted to snoop. Maybe he thought I was having an affair and planned to report it to Mom for some extra brownie points with her! Lately, his attention span seemed more erratic than his wardrobe choices.

He repeatedly offered to take me to a hospital, but for reasons I couldn't quite explain, I kept declining, caught in what felt like a panic attack. Frustrated, he finally said, "I know a guy not far from here. He deals in a special drug that'll calm your nerves." I didn't protest—partly out of curiosity, but mostly because I was in so much pain. He navigated the car toward one of the sketchiest parts of Uttara. He parked and told me to stay put while he went inside a dingy-looking building to get the goods. Sure, this was a temporary fix but good guy Ranjan, always going above and beyond.

He handed me a small pouch containing three pills. When I asked him what they were, he explained that it was a special mix of weed and a white powder. He assured me it would calm me down and help my entire body relax in about 30 minutes. I wasn't completely stupid—I knew these were highly addictive, but the chest palpitations were unbearable. I took one pill and handed the others back to him, telling him I just needed enough to calm down so I could see a doctor. He smiled, agreed, and didn't press further.

As we pulled out, Ranjan casually said, "If you need more, let me know. I can get you more." Something about that didn't sit right with me. For the first time, Ranjan didn't feel like the good guy I knew. But before I could process it any further, everything went black.

The next thing I knew, I was back home in Oldtown. Groggy and disoriented, I checked my phone to find several missed calls from Rajesh, with one text message asking, "Are you staying over tonight at mine?" I texted him back, explaining everything that had happened, and assured him I'd head to the doctor as soon as the drugs left my system. I didn't want Mom to find out and the police to get involved. Ranjan never said a word about this to anyone too.

True to my word, I went to the hospital with Mom, but after all the tests, the doctors couldn't find anything. The hospital performed some regular blood tests and heart scan and they all came out healthy. The symptoms had vanished as mysteriously as they had appeared. Diary, it couldn't have been the pill Ranjan gave me, right?

Sufi | Entry 5. Scandal

DEAR DIARY,

...

It's been a while since my last confession, and quite a lot has happened. Admittedly, the gap wasn't intentional. I hid you somewhere "safe" and promptly forgot where that was. Out of sight, out of mind—until yesterday when I stumbled upon you again. So, let's go through everything in order.

Ranjan left, saying he needed to support his family in Uttara. He mentioned knowing a guy who used to work as a community security guard back when he would wait for Sammy after school. Apparently, this guy could help him find work.

Some time back, Amjad joined us for lunch, and within the first minute, he was already bragging about how many women couldn't resist gawking at his "devilishly good looks" on his way in. Sure, Amjad. They were probably hypnotised by your pudgy belly and that rapidly expanding bald patch—an irresistible combo!

Rajesh chimed in, sarcastically though, "Amjad, you're the alpha male, man! A total king of queens!"

Amjad was oblivious to the mockery. He puffed up his chest. "Yeah, man! Oh, guess what? I met this girl named Cynthia..." he said, scrolling furiously through his phone gallery, trying to find a picture of them together where she didn't look like a red flag personified. "I think she might be the *one*! I didn't tell you guys, but I met her a month ago at the Watering Hole"

Shiro, the only one among us with actual experience in dealing with girls—and women—snorted. "Amjad, I can guarantee that anyone you met at the Watering Hole is *not* the one." Despite being in his early twenties, Amjad hung out with us kids likely seeking validation for his own insecurities.

The Watering Hole was less a nightclub and more a cesspool—a magnet for hookers, creeps, and a few unsuspecting idiots like Amjad. I'd taken Yaad there a couple of times to teach him an important life lesson: *know your predators.* The mind can't protect itself from what the eyes don't recognise, right? Naturally, none of us were old enough to be there, but I knew a guy who'd let us in through the back door for the price of a dozen eggs.

Shiro loved the place, mainly because it was crawling with middle-aged women looking for "fresh meat." Somehow, his boyish good looks made him irresistible to the kind of women who justified their predation with, "I thought he was legal since we met at a night club!" We knew it was child abuse but Shiro didn't seem to mind. He called it "maturing." Diary, what would happen if the genders were reversed?

As for Yaad and me? If anyone approached us, it was always the same—hookers. One particularly persistent woman insisted on buying Yaad a drink until I had to physically intervene and intimidate her with my sandal! Still she followed us outside, handed Yaad her visiting card, and said, "Call me when the old coot isn't around." Old coot? Me? Really? Her card just said "Berry" and a phone number.

Now, here's where it gets interesting. When Amjad finally showed us Cynthia's photo, Shiro immediately burst into laughter. He leaned over and whispered to me, "Dude, that's Berry!"

Amjad was confused as ever when he asked, "*Very* what?"

Before I could stop him, Yaad chimed in, "Isn't she the one who gave me that card?"

I kicked Yaad under the table to shut him up and asked Amjad, "She's *very* pretty, Amjad. So, what exactly makes you think she's 'the one'?"

Amjad, in all his obnoxious glory, replied, "Well, I told her all about the things I have at home and the places we go on holidays. I take her to dinner at boutique restaurants every week, she laughs at all my jokes, and we've had some amazing car sex. She's totally into me"

Shiro, barely suppressing a gag, asked, "And you didn't pay her for her 'troubles'?"

Amjad followed up with a smug reply, "I give her pocket money from time to time. She's going to be my *wifey,* after all! In fact, I am taking her out tomorrow for lunch at the grand opening of the Santa Barbara's! Dad is expanding his hotel business next-door, and I want Cynthia to be a part of it!"

Rajesh seized the moment, "Alpha dog! She already sounds like a part of your family! When's the wedding? A girl like that shouldn't be kept waiting!"

Amjad grinned. "Soon, brothers. Anyway, I only have 100 taka on me today, but my order's 120. Can you guys cover the rest?"

Without missing a beat, I replied, "Of course, Amjad. Anything for you." Meanwhile, I texted Shiro under the table: "We're going to the Watering Hole tonight. Just you and me."

That night, we slipped into the main floor of the club, navigating through the smoky haze and deafening music, all while keeping an eye out for Berry. After asking a few of the girls, one of them gestured toward a booth and said, "She's with someone right now."

Ignoring the hint, we walked over to the booth to find Berry laughing and flirting with an older gentleman. The moment the man spotted Shiro, he froze, muttered something incoherent, and hurriedly left the booth.

Confused, I turned to Shiro and asked, "What was that about?"

Shiro grinned. "Oh, that's my upstairs neighbour. He probably bolted because he didn't want me recognising him. His wife is good friends with my mom and always complains about how late he works. Guess he *was* working late... just not at the office!"

Berry, visibly annoyed by the interruption, stood up and snapped, "What do you want?"

I stepped forward and replied nonchalantly, "Let me make it worth your while. Upstairs hotel room, you and me. Nothing fancy—just one blow. I've got cash."

Shiro stared at me like I'd just grown a second head. He was right to look shocked—this wasn't me, and I definitely didn't have the money to back up the offer. I wasn't looking for anything; I was fishing for an answer.

Without missing a beat, Berry replied, "Sure."

Caught off guard by her quick agreement, I asked, "Really? That's it? No 'old coot' nonsense?"

Berry shrugged. "Money is money. Doesn't matter where it comes from."

She began leading us toward the elevator when Shiro leaned in and whispered urgently, "What the hell are you doing?!"

I whispered back, "Shut up, Shiro."

A few steps later, I stopped abruptly. "Actually Berry, on second thought, let's make it even better. Tomorrow at 1:00 pm, meet us at the Padmashetu Hotel. You know the place? It's next to Santa Barbara's. I just happen to know that Al-Giri of Al-Giri Pharmaceuticals is looking for a good time."

Berry narrowed her eyes, clearly sceptical. "You're lying and wasting my time."

From behind me, Shiro muttered under his breath, "You can say that again."

I locked eyes with Berry channelling the overconfidence of a cheating rom-con antihero trying to bed their next-door neighbour. "How sure are you about that? You might just be passing up the easiest gig of your life. The choice is yours."

Berry hesitated, checked her phone, and then looked back at me. "Fine. I'll be in the area anyway, so I'll drop by. But if you're playing me, I'm out."

"That's all I ask," I said. Then, out of curiosity, I asked, "But if you'll already be in the area, do you work around there too?"

Berry was clearly not amused. "None of your business," she snapped, before turning on her heel and marching back into the club.

As we left the club, Shiro shook his head. "That was the worst lie you've ever told, Sufi. Al-Giri? Seriously?"

I smirked. "It's not a lie if you know how to make it work. I might not know *the* Al-Giri, but I definitely know his youngest son, Ibran!"

Shiro's eyes widened. "You mean the weird fellow from the party who was always staring at people?"

"That's the one," I said. "They called him a wh*remonger. The real challenge won't be getting him to agree—it'll be getting him to agree to exactly what I need."

Shiro groaned. "This is insane and completely unnecessary."

"Trust the process," I said with a grin. "Now head home. I've got a call to make."

As Shiro left, I walked to the bus stop, pulled out my phone, and dialled Ibran.

The next day, I convinced Rajesh to lend me some money, which I used to book a room at Padmashetu Hotel under Ibran's name. I deliberately left Rajesh and Shiro out of it—this plan had the potential to spiral out of control, and I didn't want them caught in the fallout.

At exactly 12:30 pm, Berry arrived, rushing into the lobby as if she had sprinted there. She was dressed in a salwar kameez, looking more like she was heading to a formal family event than her usual line of work. Slightly out of breath, she cut to the chase, "I know you're wasting my time. I have somewhere to be, so let's get this over with. Prove me right."

Keeping a calm demeanour, I motioned for her to follow me upstairs. She refused, demanding proof before she'd take another step. Pulling out a thick stack of cash, I handed her a portion. "You'll get the rest after," I said evenly. A small part of me hoped she'd decline and walk away. But she didn't. She accepted the cash, and we headed to the room.

When Berry entered, she immediately froze in disgust. Sitting on the bed, stark naked and scrolling through his phone, was Ibran.

"Who's this?" she asked, her voice sharp.

"As I promised, Berry—Al-Giri. Or at least his youngest son," I replied, keeping my tone light.

"Is he even old enough?" she asked, clearly appalled.

I smirked. "Come on, Berry. That's not a question you usually ask. But for the record, yes, he's 20." I placed the entire bundle of cash on the bedside table. "Look, it's easy money. Just like I said yesterday—nothing fancy, just one blow. You don't even have to strip. I can even get you a bib if you don't want ibran on your clothes!"

From the bed, Ibran chimed in awkwardly, "And I get to film it too, right? You said I could?"

At that, Berry bristled. "I'm not agreeing to that!"

"That's entirely up to you," I said nonchalantly. "But its easy money. Besides, do you really think Ibran would leak the video? His dad would kill him for shaming the family name. And if you impress him, maybe he'll make you his regular."

Ibran nodded eagerly. His face showed a mixture of embarrassment and excitement.

Berry hesitated, her gaze darting between the thick bundle of cash and the door. Finally, she walked over to the bedside table, stuffed the money into her bag, and set it aside. Without another word, she knelt in front of Ibran and began the deed. He, of course, started filming immediately, the creep. I stood at the corner of the room observing.

Halfway through, I reminded her, "Don't forget to swallow."

As the clock struck 1:00 pm, Berry's phone began ringing incessantly. I asked, "Do you need to take that?" but she ignored me, increasing her pace like she was racing the clock.

When Ibran finished, Berry stood up, visibly flustered, with some of Ibran's *'children'* over her lips. She made for the bathroom to clean up. I quickly stepped in front of the door. "Oh, sorry. The bathroom's out of service. You might want to freshen up elsewhere—you've got places to be, right?"

Berry glared at me but said nothing. She grabbed her bag and stormed out, her phone still buzzing as she left. *I wonder if Amjad will taste Ibran on her when he leans in for a kiss today,* I thought with a smirk!

After she stormed out, Ibran, still catching his breath, wasted no time replaying the video on his phone. His eyes lit up with a perverse satisfaction as he turned to me and said, "You're right! It hits different when the girl looks all formal, like she's off-limits. There's just something about doing it with someone who seems unavailable instead of one flaunting herself to reel you in."

I couldn't help but roll my eyes at his twisted logic. "Get dressed," I snapped, walking out of the room before he could say anything else. I wished Berry had proven me wrong.

A year went by. I completed my O-level exams, and to Yaad's credit as a tutor, I did fairly well. Nothing earth-shattering, but still commendable. I now found myself neck-deep in preparation for my final Year 12 A-level exams. *Nanu* underwent chemotherapy as new scans revealed that the cancer had spread to her brain. These updates were heavy on my heart, but I focused on what I could control: studying. I knew this was my last chance to make something of myself. My grades hadn't been stellar, so a scholarship to study at a university degree overseas was out of the question.

Despite my best efforts, the pressure mounted, and my health began to deteriorate. As the exam dates drew nearer, my heart palpitations worsened, each beat a reminder of the growing tension. Diary, you don't have a body so you wouldn't know, but the human body has a strange way of manifesting stress, almost as if it's crafting an escape route from the pressure of being unprepared. I couldn't help but wonder if that's what was happening to me—was this just my body's clever way of inventing an excuse for my shortcomings? It reminds me of how some of the girls in class would don hijabs during practical exams, using religion as a shield to curry favour with the more religious examiners, only to toss the hijabs aside afterward and flaunt their newly highlighted hair. Then there were those who always seemed to fall ill right before their turn in the practical assessment, conveniently asking the examiners to go easy on them. I couldn't shake the feeling that my body was trying to place me in that second category!

Most days, I stayed at Yaad's place. After his sister left the country and his dad moved out, I began crashing in his dad's old room, making a makeshift bed on the floor. Plus, Yaad's caretaker, Anna, made the best chicken nuggets I'd ever had! Yaad asked me to sell his car, but I had a feeling he might regret it later. Instead of outright refusing, I concocted a ridiculous story about knowing someone who could chop up the car and sell it for parts. The lie wasn't even remotely convincing, but somehow, it worked.

One day, while we were studying, that familiar chest pain and restlessness crept in. It wasn't unbearable, but it was distracting enough to keep me from focusing. Going to the hospital hadn't helped in the past—they'd just admit me and waste time I didn't have. I don't know what made me think it was a good idea, but I decided to step out and give Ranjan a call for one of his "magic pills" that had seemed to work before. I convinced myself I'd see a doctor after the exams... the same excuse every addict makes on their path to dependency.

When I called, his number was no longer in service. Frustrated, I impulsively messaged Rajesh and Shiro: "I'm heading to my weed dealer's place to get a fix. Rajesh knows where to find me." Then I hailed a rickshaw and went to the dingy four-story building Ranjan had once taken me to.

The place reeked of desperation. I knocked on a door on one of the floors, and a woman answered. Her sunken eyes and frail demeanour screamed addiction, but she insisted she was a nurse and didn't know what I was talking about. Then, almost as an afterthought, she hinted that I should check the floor upstairs.

As I climbed the stairs, I heard a door creak open behind me and noticed an older, overweight man descending, giving me a sly, knowing glance as he passed. When I reached the next floor, a pale, young woman was closing her door. She paused, eyeing me cautiously, and asked, "Yes? Do you need something?"

I stumbled over my words, unsure of what to say. Then, to my relief, Ranjan appeared behind her. "Sufi, what are you doing here?" he asked surprised. He was dressed in a simple t-shirt and sarong, with a silver chain around his neck—a far cry from the flamboyant outfits he wears outdoors. It was clear he was at home.

I told him about the chest palpitations and sweating, explaining that they were getting out of control again. I needed one of his miracle fixes.

Ranjan sighed and let me in, introducing the pale young woman as "Riba," his sister. She looked to be in the final trimester of pregnancy. I asked when she was due, but she didn't respond. Instead, she quietly retreated to a room and shut the door. Her behaviour reminded me of Sammy—withdrawn and awkward.

As I stood in the corridor, my attention was drawn to another partially open door nearby. Peering inside, I saw two young girls sitting on worn mattresses spread across the floor. There was something oddly familiar about them, though I couldn't quite place where I'd seen them before. Before I could gather my thoughts or say anything, one of them suddenly jumped up and shut the door on my face. The last thing I noticed was the faint outline of a scar running along her cheek—poor girl.

Ranjan walked to a room at the far end of the corridor, and I heard the sound of a cabinet opening, followed by small, bare footsteps as he asked someone in a childish tone to move aside. I stood awkwardly in the middle of the hallway, my attention drawn to a locked door next to me. The padlock on it was old, with a red accent stripe. Faint groaning noises came from inside—someone in pain, perhaps. Ranjan clearly had his hands full here!

Ranjan returned with a pack of just one pill and walked me out. "If you need more, call me first. But Sufi, you need to see a doctor for that." he said.

"I tried calling, but your number's disconnected," I replied.

"Oh. I've got your number. I'll ring you later when you're feeling better so you can save my new contact. Don't take the pill until you're home, or you might pass out on the way."

"What do I owe you?" I asked, feeling guilty.

"Nothing," he said. "Just take care of yourself."

It was clear now—Ranjan was the dealer here. A part of me wanted to turn him in, to put an end to everything, but seeing how he was caring for his sisters, an unborn child, and whoever else was in that house made me hesitate. Who would look after them if he were gone?

I left and headed back to Yaad's place. There was no point in telling him where I'd been—he'd only worry about my health. I told him I was tired and needed some sleep. In my makeshift room, I popped the pill and slowly drifted into oblivion which didn't seem to do the trick as well as it did the first time.

A week before my A-level exams, I decided to head back home to Oldtown. I figured Yaad needed some peace and quiet to focus on his final preparations without having to babysit me all the time.

One afternoon, just two days before my upcoming biology exam, I sat at my desk reviewing my notes on yeast culture, when the room suddenly started spinning. I instinctively rushed to the small window in my room, desperate for air, but the house next door had installed an air conditioner that blew warm, suffocating air straight into my window.

The heat seemed to thicken the air around me, and I started sweating, my heart pounding harder.

I barely made it to the door when my head spun violently, and I collapsed just outside my room. The last thing I saw before everything went dark was Mahi rushing toward me as Nessa stood curiously at the corner of my vision. When I woke up, I was in a hospital bed. Mom sat beside me, with an expression mixed with worry and relief.

I looked at Mom with more guilt than relief. "I'm sorry for pulling you away from work."

She shook her head gently. "Don't say that. Besides, I've been here since yesterday."

"Yesterday?!" I exclaimed, taken aback. "I was asleep all night?"

She nodded, and it suddenly hit me. "That means my exam is tomorrow!"

Mom's face softened. "Let's focus on getting you better first. The doctors ran a few tests while you were unconscious, and we're still waiting for the results."

I tried sounding not desperate. "I can take the exam and come back afterward!"

She looked at me, understanding my urgency. "If you can convince the doctor when he sees you this evening, I'll support you."

With a bit of effort and a sleazy marketing pitch, I managed to do just that. Though hesitant, the doctor finally agreed—on the condition that my mother sign a waiver releasing the hospital from liability. The next morning, we left the hospital and headed straight to the exam venue.

While I'd love to say everything was fine, it wasn't. Halfway through the exam, the same symptoms hit me again. My heart raced, and I started sweating profusely. The room spun so violently at times that I had to lay my head down on the desk just to steady myself. But I refused to tell the exam invigilators—I didn't want anyone to think I was making excuses.

That afternoon, I returned to the hospital to collect my test results. Routine checks on my heart, liver, kidney, and blood function all came back normal. The doctors suggested I stay a few more days for observation, but I declined. I couldn't afford to lose more time and the costs of the tests would add more strain to Mom and her family who were already struggling to support *Nanu*'s compounding cost of care.

The day after my exams ended was total chaos.

I got a call from Ibran, sounding panicked. "You have to help, bro. She refuses to be recorded anymore!"

I was caught off guard. "What? I don't understand."

He hurriedly explained, "Berry! We met at the hotel just like always, but she says she no longer wants to be recorded."

I shot back, "why is that...No, *how* is this my problem?"

He replied, "She's threatening to file a lawsuit for sexual assault if I don't delete all the videos!"

I found it quite amusing. "Ibran, what did you do?"

He almost sounded convincing, "I swear, nothing, man! She stayed quiet as long as it was convenient for her, and now she's speaking out when it's no longer. Please, come over and talk to her. I don't know who else to call."

I asked, "Come over where?"

He told me he was holed up at the Padmashetu *International* Hotel—rebranded as if slapping the word "International" on it made it sound more credible.

I decided to take a different approach. "What do I get for talking her down?"

Ibran, desperate, replied, "Anything, man! Anything."

I went to the hotel, knocked on the door, and found Berry standing there, fully dressed in formal attire, while Ibran sat hunched on the bed, looking defeated. Their rendezvous had clearly gone sideways.

Berry said, "This has gone on long enough. Make that little pervert delete everything he has recorded!"

I turned to Ibran. "Did you hurt her?"

He quickly shot back, "I never harmed a hair on her body that she didn't consent to."

I looked at Berry, "Well?"

She replied, "If you don't make him delete all the videos, I'll sue him and take his family business down with him!"

Ibran, terrified, added, "See! She's blackmailing me!"

I addressed Berry again, "Berry, every time you took the cash, you consented to his terms. If you want to back out now, give him his money back, and we'll talk."

Ibran, still cornered, piped up, "That sounds fair! I'll not be unreasonable. I'll accept half of the payment returned!"

I knew it would be impossible for Berry to return all the money she'd spent. It would be easier for her to play the victim and threaten a lawsuit, knowing the legal system would likely side with her. Ibran didn't stand a chance.

I asked, "Why are you doing this now? What's changed?"

Berry went silent, but I already knew. The answer was sitting in my social media inbox—Amjad had invited me to his wedding with Cynthia. So, Berry's real name was Cynthia after all.

I took a deep breath and took charge. "Look, Berry, I know you're getting married to Amjad. You probably don't want this to stain your reputation with his family. The more you make a scene here, the more I'm tempted to let Ibran send everything he's recorded to Amjad. Now, you can choose: leave now and never look back, or keep messing with the guy in the corner and risk losing your chance at a happy ending."

Berry silently walked out, and I turned to Ibran, who couldn't stop thanking me. "What do you want for helping me out?" he asked.

Before I could answer, my phone buzzed with a message from Yaad. His dad had crashed and was fighting for his life at the hospital.

I glanced at Ibran, his fanny pack full of cash in front of me. A thought struck me, and I asked, "How much money did you bring today?"

He pulled out a thick bundle of cash. Without hesitation, I took the entire bundle and said, "Consider this my payment," before walking out and heading straight to Kuddus Memorial Hospital.

At the hospital, Yaad refused to accept my payment and insisted I leave. I held onto the money for a few more weeks, unsure what to do with it, until Nida, his sister, arrived back in Bangladesh to care for their father. I decided to give it to her, knowing they were still reeling from the sudden crisis with their dad. Though she hesitated, I used my best "used car salesman" pitch to convince her it was a loan, making her promise not to tell Yaad. The truth was, I didn't intend to ever ask for the money back. I just wanted to help in the only way I knew how.

The next day, I got a call from Amjad. He was inviting me and the boys to a gathering before his wedding—a morally sanitised version of a bachelor party, perhaps. Rajesh and I agreed to go, though Shiro chose to sit this one out.

The event was at Amjad's sprawling estate on the outskirts of the city. He greeted us at the door with his usual enthusiasm, introducing us to his parents and his sister, Ayesha, who had flown in to attend the wedding.

Rajesh was never one to filter his sarcastic thoughts. He asked, "Alpha dog! Where's your queen-to-be?"

Amjad chuckled, "Not tonight!". His fiancée was busy helping her in-laws with her dream wedding preparations—or rather, the five extravagant events planned to celebrate their union. Weddings like these baffled me. Diary, why would anyone waste obscene amounts of money on fleeting grandeur that people you don't even properly know will criticise regardless. That money could be invested into building a stable future for the bride and groom. But, to each their own.

Amjad was buzzing with excitement, and Ayesha seemed genuinely happy to share in her brother's joy. It was clear she adored him. Later that night, Ayesha and her friends proposed heading to their family-owned hotel, the Padmashetu, for a proper celebration on the penthouse floor. Against my better judgment, we went.

While the others indulged in drinks and other vices, I stayed sober, quietly observing the dynamics. Ayesha was visibly close to Amjad, playing the role of the doting sister, while her friends spiralled into drunken revelry. Rajesh and I left early, intending to return to Memorial Hospital to support Yaad during his difficult time. However, on the way back, my chest palpitations flared up again, so severely this time that Rajesh had to drive me to a local hospital. They sedated me, ran a series of tests, and—unsurprisingly—found nothing wrong. The doctors wanted to keep me overnight, but I insisted on returning to a neighbourhood I was familiar with. I asked Rajesh to drop me home in Oldtown. By the time I arrived, I was already groggy from the sedatives. Mom guided me to my room, where I passed out, this time for nearly an entire day.

Over the following days, the chest palpitations and restlessness became more frequent. Mom took me to the nearest public hospital, but the waiting time for an admission was weeks. In the meantime, the outpatient department doctors prescribed sedatives to manage the episodes. Those pills kept me subdued for hours on end. Time became a blur, and I lost touch with everything and everyone, including Yaad and the boys. For nearly two weeks, I was disconnected, drifting in and out of awareness, until the palpitations mysteriously vanished again—and just like that, I didn't need admission after all.

When I finally came to, the boys filled me in on everything I'd missed. Yaad's family was entangled in a legal battle with Al-Giri, who was trying to steal their inheritance through falsified lawsuits. They'd been calling me repeatedly during that time, but I hadn't answered a single call. Thankfully, Rajesh and Shiro stepped up in my absence.

They told me they had gone first to Pirojpur, and then to "my dealer's" building in Uttara looking for answers, accompanied by a child named Beebo—what an absurd name! The boys knew better than to pry too deeply, respecting the family's privacy while assuring them that help was just minutes away if needed. That's the Rajesh and Shiro I knew—solid lads through and through. While I couldn't directly help, I thought I might persuade Ibran to convince his corrupt father to back off.

When I met Ibran, he was distracted—completely fixated on Berry. He had fallen for her, proving that repeated sex and exploring sexual kinks is rarely ever just sex. He wouldn't listen to a word about Yaad's situation.

I saw an opportunity to be "diplomatic!"

I suggested, "If you're so in love with her and upset she's marrying someone else, why not do something about it? She clearly values her reputation with her in-laws and wouldn't want to be caught with a pervert like you."

That lit a fire in him, just as I hoped it would. "I'll show them how much she enjoyed a 'pervert' like me!" he declared.

Within a day, the fool had leaked a year's worth of videos of himself and Berry, including the first time I introduced them. All I had to do was forward the link to the very first video to Amjad. The so-called "alpha dog" was mortified to discover he had been thoroughly "beta-ed" and cucked by someone like Ibran, who even had the audacity flip the camera to film his own expressions mid-act.

Amjad called me over, panicking and depressed. Of course, I went over being the genuinely concerned friend that I was! He couldn't show the videos to his family without bringing them immense shame, and he could no longer face Cynthia after confronting her. She confessed everything. I advised him to do whatever he thought was right and left it at that. On my way out, I might have "accidentally" dropped a green pack of "ya ba" pills onto the tea table in front of Amjad. *How did those get there?* —I thought aloud but didn't bother picking them back up!

In the end, Amjad called off the wedding. Berry retaliated in frustration, suing Ibran and the entire Al-Giri family for sexual harassment and a host of other charges. Ibran, in all his infinite wisdom, had never recorded her accepting money—only the degrading acts he made her perform that frequently made Berry cry mid act. The court, naturally, sided with Berry. Given the notoriously slow pace of the legal system in Bangladesh, the proceedings were expected to drag on for the next 10 to 20 years before reaching a final resolution.

The fallout was catastrophic. Overwhelmed by stress and isolation, Ibran fell prey to extremist recruiters who exploited his vulnerability. He spiralled into radicalism, posting provocative content online, which added another layer of disgrace to Hossein Al-Giri.

Though they won the lawsuit against Yaad's family, Al-Giri's personal life crumbled. His son required rehab and constant monitoring to prevent him from doing something reckless. The Padmashetu was dragged into the scandal and was labelled a "hotel brothel," tarnishing its reputation beyond repair. Amjad became a drug addict and was stripped of his inheritance, which was significantly less than the billion dollars which he claimed it to be, and Ayesha was forced to return and take over the family business where the locals started calling her the madame of the brothel.

Now burdened with the responsibility of managing a failing hotel, Ayesha also had to care for her disgraced brother, who was grappling with addiction. He would periodically check into the hotel under fake names, using it as a hideout while sourcing "ya ba" from their own stash. Ayesha withdrew from all social gatherings and, according to a guy I know, started drinking heavily, and even spent several nights in prison for drink driving. It's probably only a matter of time before the once vibrant and impeccably styled fashionista turns into a dishevelled alcoholic, struggling to hold onto even a shadow of her former self—enough to make any man turn and run away.

This one's for you, Sammy.

I introduced Yaad to Mom, and she immediately took a liking to him, saying he reminded her of Sammy. I agreed. Before meeting in person, they had spoken a few times over the phone, with Mom guiding him on cooking when he lived alone.

Amid university admissions and my own health issues, I gradually lost touch with Rajesh and Shiro. But Fridays were different. Every Friday, Yaad would visit us in Oldtown, sharing lunch with Mom and me. As the weeks went by, Yaad and Mom became increasingly comfortable with each other. After two months, they were so at ease that he would lie on Mom's lap, sharing the details of his week while she gently ran her fingers through his hair until he drifted off to sleep. Those moments were rare glimpses of peace. Before he left in the afternoons, *Nanu* always packed food for him.

Sometimes, my mamas and khalas joined us, filling the room with lively and thought-provoking conversations. The warmth and laughter reminded me of better times. Every Thursday, Yaad would call Mom and cheerfully remind her, "Tomorrow is Friday." It became her beacon of joy in an otherwise monotonous week.

"What would you like me to prepare for you, Yaad?" she'd ask.

"Could you please make me some roasted chicken, Aunty?" Yaad would respond, knowing her well enough to request her signature dish.

"Absolutely," she'd always say, her tone brightening. "I'll head to the grocer and get everything. You must be tired now, so rest well. We'll see you tomorrow." Like clockwork, the same exchange played out every week for almost four months.

During his visits, Mom would share stories about Sammy's ambitions and read poems from her English Literature days, just as she once did for Sammy and me. Meanwhile, Yaad and I would dive into intense chess sessions. Interestingly, we both had a habit of heavily relying on the knight, making our matches all the more unpredictable and engaging. Mom ended up planting the notion of pursuing higher education in him, insisting he had the intellect to make a difference.

Yaad's presence brought a spark of joy to Mom that I hadn't seen in years, and it eased some of my worries. He finished school before I did, having excelled at everything while I struggled, failing year 12. Yaad was accepted into Medicine in Sylhet, one step closer to realising Sammy's dreams—and I knew I wanted to follow suit. I couldn't help but feel that Mom's influence had helped guide him onto this path, and that brought me some comfort. For a moment, it felt like Sammy was with us again, even if it were for a little while.

Sufi | Entry 6. Karma

DIARY,

...

I thought it was time to update you on what's happened in the six years since Sammy—no, Yaad left for university across the country.

Mom moved out of *Nanu's* home and subleased a room closer to her workplace. The long commute and relentless traffic had begun taking a toll on her health. She suggested I stay back with *Nanu* and the rest of the family, but I had my own aspirations to chase: Sammy's dream of becoming a doctor, and though I doubted I'd ever be smart enough to pursue a PhD, I wanted to at least try and follow in her footsteps.

I was determined to explore the path of dentistry after I saw how it helped Sammy regain some of her confidence and helped her smile a little. I sought advice from Yaad who already started his degree. He patiently walked me through the admission process. He told me that in Bangladesh, clinical health courses like medicine and dentistry were centralised under one exam. The exam had two components, an 'earned marks' component that provided a score based on my O and A-level results, and a 'written exam' component. The universities then ranked candidates based on their scores and selected the top students for interviews.

I wasn't as smart as Yaad. To give me the best fighting chance, Mom quickly enrolled me in a health preparatory course at Farmgate, one of the busiest and most chaotic parts of the city. Farmgate was known for its bustling markets and as a hub for university admissions coaching. The place was also notorious for being a hotspot where criminals preyed on naïve, young students arriving from rural areas to prepare for their exams.

To keep me focused and out of trouble, Mom "locked" me up in her subleased room for days at a stretch, which was closer to Farmgate than

Nanu's place in Oldtown. She'd leave for work, making sure I had all the food and supplies I needed so that I could focus solely on studying for the exam. It was tough on Mom. But she never once complained. In fact, she encouraged me. "Don't look back," she'd say. "Make something of yourself and get out!"

I spent most of my time in Mom's subleased room, making a bed on the floor and studying beside it. I'd turned that small corner of the floor into a makeshift study area. When it was time to go back to Oldtown at the end of the week, the commute from Oldtown to Farmgate was a nightmare. After the preparatory course lectures wrapped up at 5:00 pm, I found myself battling for space on the public buses, crammed in shoulder to shoulder with office workers. More often than not, I'd end up with my face uncomfortably close to sweaty armpits, all of us just trying to make our way home after a long day! More than once, I was elbowed in the chest while trying to get on the bus, knocking me off balance and sending me to the ground. No one stopped to help—everyone was in too much of a rush to battle the traffic, often three hours long, to get home to their loved ones.

Pickpockets were always on the lookout, and I'd witnessed people getting their wallets stolen countless times. I didn't intervene—I'd simply let the victim know what had happened, which usually caused them to get off and chase the thief. I know it sounds selfish, but this tactic opened up a spot on the bus for me. Besides, there was a high chance he would have elbowed me anyway! It was survival mode for the working class in Bangladesh, where cars were still a luxury of the upper middle class. Public transport in Dhaka is not for beginners, Diary!

Despite all the obstacles, I threw myself into preparing for the national health exams. I poured every ounce of energy into it, hoping to turn things around. Yet, the tutors at the preparatory centre were relentless in their pessimism. No matter how well I performed in the written exams, they insisted that my school grades would drag me down in such a competitive field. According to them, the only way I could make it was if I scored the highest in the country that year.

What stressed me out was the constant belittling I endured at the preparatory centre, where the mentors seemed to relish reminding me that I stood no chance of succeeding. I might have taken their words as constructive criticism if they had offered any viable alternatives—but they never did. It's ironic how easily anyone can become a mentor after clearing an exam that has hundreds of variations to its questions. A mentor who passes one version of the test is deemed qualified to teach the entire syllabus, yet some present themselves as experts in the exam's entirety. There really should be a disclaimer: clearing a professional exam doesn't make someone an academic authority for the exam. It only certifies that they succeeded in one of many potential iterations.

Medical admissions exam day came and went without much fanfare. I was satisfied with my performance, but deep down, I knew it would take a miracle to score high enough to secure an interview. With so much free time on my hands, I decided to spend some of it with my *Nanu*, who had grown quieter but remained the kind-hearted person I had always loved. As time went on, our contact diminished. Yaad grew busy with his own studies and work, while I settled into my mother's small room. I realised that home wasn't a place—it was the people, and for me, that was my mother, Sammy, *Nanu*, cousins, and everyone who genuinely cared for me.

Things felt peaceful—for the moment, at least—until the exam results were due in a month. When the results finally came out, I didn't make it. But that didn't mean I was going to give up. I immediately began preparing for the next year's exam. After all, we were allowed a maximum of two attempts in one lifetime, and what kind of person would I be if I gave up after just one failure? Crying over a single setback wasn't my style. So, I put my head down, studied harder, and took the exam again around the same time the following year.

One morning, a text notification arrived from the government: the results were out. My heart pounded as I logged on to the results portal, already bracing myself for disappointment. And there it was—exactly what I had feared. While I had scored among the top in the written exam, my previous grades from school dragged me down significantly, just as everyone had warned. I felt gutted. My experience felt more like a confirmation of the naysayers' opinions—like they're all high-fiving each other and saying, "We told you so!" It's not a perfect system. It's a global problem that probably won't get fixed until we sort out hunger, global warming, and world peace. Honestly, I believe we have a better shot at tackling global warming than at resolving bureaucratic mismanagement in academia, largely because it lacks the funding and spotlight. After all, how many Miss Universe winners have graced the stage and proclaimed, "I want less bureaucracy in academia!" compared to those who say, "I want world peace!"?

I called Mom to break the news. Her response was calm: "This doesn't stop us from applying to the universities, does it?"

"No, but the public schools won't take me," I said, my voice flat with resignation.

"What about the private institutions?" she asked.

"They're too expensive. I couldn't possibly—"

She cut me off. "Don't forget, we have the money from the property your *Nanu* sold. I'm not taking it with me to the grave, so let me do this for you, please."

Private institutions weren't just about rankings; they considered extracurricular activities, financial ability, and other factors like...erm political lobbying! I applied to several private dental schools in Dhaka, many operating as extensions of the University of Dhaka's dental curriculum, given the university's limited clinical facilities. Some admission clerks outright rejected my application, saying I stood no chance. Others hinted at bribes just to get my application reviewed. Reluctantly, we chose the lesser of two evils, knowing that paying the bribe wouldn't guarantee admission—just a chance for my application to be seen. It's similar to how, if I wanted to sell my samosas on an e-commerce platform, I'd have to pay to boost my product's visibility just to reach the right audience. It's not necessary, but with so many other samosa sellers competing for attention, it becomes a gamble whether my samosas get noticed at all. Both systems involve middlemen profiting from someone else's hard work, while relying on their industry connections to improve your chances at opening a door that would otherwise remain shut.

In my applications, I emphasised every extracurricular activity that I had participated in, but I prepared myself for the likely outcome that the call would never come. To pass the time, I even began exploring other career options—like watching paint dry! Then, one afternoon, the unexpected happened—a dental school called and invited me for an interview. I was baffled. Why me?

At the interview, one of the assessors looked at my cover letter and remarked, "You're aware that your ranking isn't quite on par with many of the other applicants, right?"

"Yes, ma'am," I replied.

She smiled. "That said, I noticed you took some interesting extracurricular classes in school. Could you tell me more about those?"

"I did Karate for a while ma'am, until our instructor fell off a tree..." I started explaining before one of the panel members stopped me. "We meant art and stitching handwork!"

"Oh!" I exclaimed, "I can do complex stitches, and I can draw...erm...the human anatomy well"

She nodded, still smiling. "Yes."

I went on to explain my experiences making quilt covers and selling pillows at school, watching as the board of three smiled and jotted down notes.

Two weeks later, the results were posted outside the admissions office. I pushed through the crowd of students to look at the board, scanning the list of names. My heart skipped a beat. I had made it into dentistry!

Here's the thing about dentistry—it's a unique blend of aesthetics, precision, and academic skill. A sense of artistic proportion, combined with the ability to handle sharp instruments with finesse, is highly valued in the field.

I moved in with Mom full time, settling into her small, one-bedroom sublet. I made my bed and study area on the floor beside her bed—a practical, cost-effective solution until we could afford to rent an additional room in the coming years. I set everything up carefully, organising my modest space, and then waited for classes to begin.

Orientation day arrived, and I was introduced to a diverse array of new faces. One standout was Pinto, who seemed entirely disinterested in studying dentistry, pursuing it solely due to family pressure. He shared some of his passions such as playing the violin and bodybuilding—a fascinating combination! After the orientation seminar, Pinto invited me to his "spot" in the city to hang out that afternoon. I cautiously asked, "Sure, can I bring a friend?" I didn't know Pinto very well yet, and while I was somewhat familiar with the neighbourhood, I wasn't confident about the specific area he was inviting me to, so I felt that having a friend will keep me at ease.

"Absolutely! I'll invite some of my friends too," Pinto replied.

As I exited the orientation hall, I reached out via phone to the biggest guy I knew, who also happened to lived nearby. I had met him through Rajesh, who affectionately called him "Rhino" due to his imposing 195 cm stature and muscular build. At least it was better than "Alpha dog!" Rhino had an insatiable love for food and would do anything for a good meal. When I called him at 1:00 pm, he picked up still half-asleep.

"Rhino!" I exclaimed, "I met some friends in dental school, and they want me to hang out with them in a part of the city I'm not familiar with. Can you come with me? I'll buy you one of Dhaka's favourite mayo-drenched burgers afterward."

"Sure! Come over to my place, and we'll head out together," he replied, still groggy.

I made my way to his home and rang the doorbell. When Rhino opened the door, he was dressed in a snug polo shirt and shorts, his bulging tummy barely contained. He cracked his knuckles and exclaimed in his deep voice, "Let's go beat up some nerds, man!"

I quickly clarified, "We're not going to pick a fight, Rhino!"

It was as if my words flew right over his head. He bounded downstairs and hailed a rickshaw. As he climbed in, the rickshaw-puller was nearly lifted off the ground by Rhino's sheer weight, forcing him to step back and readjust the vehicle.

"Hop on, man! I know a great mayo burger joint that serves extra mayonnaise on the side. We can hit it up after we're done," Rhino said. His enthusiasm at beating some helpless students up felt infectious.

"Remember, we're just hanging out," I reiterated as I climbed into the rickshaw, which creaked under our weight. The lean rickshaw-puller struggled to gain momentum, moving at a snail's pace. I couldn't help but think that I should have opted for an auto-rickshaw instead!

We arrived at a location that resembled an abandoned seven-story building. Its construction had been long forgotten. Rhino squinted at the structure and whispered, "Is it the building next to the one under construction?"

"Hold on; let me call and confirm," I replied, dialling Pinto. He confirmed we were at the right place and instructed us to head straight to the roof.

As we climbed the unrailed staircase, I could see Rhino's bravado begin to wane. "I don't like this one bit, man," he muttered, sounding almost like a scared child. By the time we reached the rooftop, I was fine, but Rhino was completely out of breath, gasping as he tried to regain his composure.

I spotted Pinto and five other guys gathered in one corner, drinking beverages and snacking on chips. As they saw us, they all stood up and walked over to greet us.

Here's the thing: Pinto's friends were all from the gym he frequented, and they were built like tanks. Rhino's eyes widened in fear, and he whispered again, "These aren't nerds, man!"

I turned to him, annoyed. "I never said they were! Where did you get that idea?"

"I don't know, man. When you mentioned you met them at orientation, I thought... you know... doctors... nerds?"

Ignoring Rhino's crude stereotyping, I faced the group as they approached, each offering a firm handshake while introducing themselves. When it was Rhino's turn, he repeated his name after each introduction, his voice growing more strained with every handshake. By the time he reached the fifth guy, his deep voice had morphed into a high-pitched squeak as he said, "Rhino..."

Pinto stared at us, eyes wide, and asked, "Is 'Rhino' your legal name?"

Rhino squeaked, "No."

Pinto let out a laugh, shaking his head. "I've never met anyone who introduces themselves as 'Rhino' to a complete stranger."

Rhino glanced at me, his eyes wide, and said in that same squeaky voice, "I left something at home that I should go get."

And just like that, Rhino bolted down the stairs, leaving me alone with six bewildered strangers, all equally confused about what had just transpired.

Pinto offered me a selection of snacks, which I politely declined. Then, the six guys beckoned me to join them in a corner.

"What are you guys up to?" I asked, half-jokingly thinking the worst they might do was toss me off the roof!

To my surprise, Pinto replied, "We were about to play chess!" My mouth fell open in disbelief as he continued, "But the boys don't want to play with me anymore because I'm too good! So... care to play?"

It had been a while since my last game, but I thought, "*why not? This might just be my last game before I'm tossed off the roof!*"

We set up the chessboard on the floor while his friends lounged nearby, chatting among themselves, completely uninterested in our game.

Pinto was an aggressive player. From the very start, it felt like the game was stacked against me. I lost most of my pawns early on, and my queen was taken within the first few moves, leaving my position looking dangerously weak. Or at least, that's what it seemed like.

Curiously, he asked, "So, what's your favourite chess piece?"

I answered, "The knight."

He chuckled, "A knight!? A queen is so much more useful. Why would anyone choose a knight?"

I moved my knight over the pawn in front of it, positioning it strategically, and replied, "They're not blocked by what's in front of them."

Pinto mocked, "They can't even move straight or hit something directly in front of them!"

I brushed off his taunts and changed the topic, "You said you didn't want to study dentistry?"

"No, man, I didn't want to study medicine either. But my family kept pushing me, saying my only options were to become a doctor or an engineer. They made it clear that, at the very least, I had to become a dentist to carry on the family tradition of becoming the next in a long line of doctors," he responded.

Recognising this was a common mindset among parents of that generation, I asked, "So what do you want to do for a living?"

Pinto replied quickly, "I like gardening. The smell of fresh herbs is amazing!"

Who would have guessed?

"So would you have preferred to do something like horticulture?" I asked.

"No man, I wanted to be a chef! A Pâtissier more specifically! Cook by day, play my violin by night."

"Didn't you try to tell them?" I asked.

Pinto responded immediately, "Look, man, I knew they wouldn't listen. My mom laughed when first I told her I wanted to learn to play the violin years ago. She said my hands were too big for it and suggested I find something more "manly" instead...still mocks me to this day! So, this time I devised an elaborate plan: I decided to leave my engineering and medical exam papers blank and fail. Sure enough, I bombed the engineering admissions tests, but when I sat for the medical exam, I don't know what happened. I knew all the answers, and my fingers were just itching to mark them down, so I did!"

I followed up, "And you got in. Clearly, you're good at it!"

Pinto shrugged. "Just because you're good at something doesn't mean you enjoy it! I'm great at cutting meat into perfect slices, but that doesn't mean I'd want to work at a slaughterhouse, putting down hundreds of animals every day. Cooking, though? I'm good at it, and I love every bit of it."

I nodded and asked him to continue, "Then what happened?"

"When the results came out, I got in. But I didn't want to. I planned an elaborate three-course meal for my family with a beautiful cake at the end to show them where my true passion lay!"

I raised an eyebrow. "Did that work?"

Pinto shook his head, a wry smile forming on his lips. "No! It backfired! They thought I was so happy about getting into dentistry that I went out of my way to cook for them, completely oblivious to everything else."

I smiled nodded, and we returned to the game. My knights were sacrificed as I intentionally played haphazardly, only confirming Pinto's impression of me as a novice. But as he gained a significant material advantage, he became overconfident. That was my cue. I'd been taught in chess to give your opponent what they want and only take what you need.

In his eagerness to capture my valuable pieces, Pinto left his king exposed, with only his queen protecting it. Seizing the opportunity, I moved my remaining rook into a strategic position, separating the queen from her king and limiting its mobility. I then advanced my bishop, blocking the king's escape routes. Pinto scrambled to protect his queen, attempting to move it further away from the threat of my rook. That was it. I swiftly moved my knight, which had been sitting idle, as it leapt it over my bishop, cornering both his king and queen. Separated from each other, they were at the mercy of my knight, unable to defend themselves from its reach. "Checkmate!" I declared

Pinto's friends looked at him, then erupted in laughter. His eyes widened in disbelief. I felt a rush of terror, thinking, "*This is it... I'm going off the roof!*"

But in an instant, his shock faded. He extended his arm for a handshake and said, "And here I thought knights were only good for being cannon fodder! Well played, friend!"

Pinto resumed the conversation we were having outside of chess. "I have a few things planned. I'll try failing the first year once; they're bound to notice."

"That's a bad idea," I replied. "Both financially and in terms of the time you'd be wasting."

"But I'll be doing other things!" he insisted. "I'll set up a food cart that sells burgers and fries down the street with the boys. We'll all pitch in and we'll hire someone to do the cooking and selling while I am in class! And when the business grows, I'll surprise my folks by showing them I'm an entrepreneur!"

I couldn't help but recall how every Tom, Dick, and Harry was riding the junk food wave at that time, including me until *someone* ate all my samosas!

"I don't think that's a good plan," I said.

He looked confused. "Do you think I should try another business? Maybe selling beauty products?" He misunderstood my hesitance as a critique of his food idea.

I replied, "That's not what I meant. I meant tell them that you want to do that instead of pursuing dentistry"

To which Pinto concluded, "It's never that simple!"

Looking back now, I know that Pinto ultimately decided to pursue dentistry. He failed at least once each year, taking gap years in between as he secretly jumped from one failed business idea to another. He finally confessed at home why he did what he did, who later supported him as he left dentistry behind to pursue his true passion for culinary arts overseas. He tried so hard to conform to societal expectations without ever letting anyone know what he truly wanted.

From Pinto, I understood the value of keeping it simple. We often romanticise our goals, imagining them as complex or out of reach. This mindset leads us to overcomplicate situations with excuses, blaming external factors for our inaction. In the end, we are the ones who lose out, and no amount of complaining can recover a missed opportunity, or the time lost.

Ironically, this lesson proved the hardest to follow, especially when others didn't share the same mindset. The real challenge with simplicity is that, even when you try to streamline your approach, your goals or work are often intertwined with others—colleagues, partners, or collaborators—who may complicate things. When someone else chooses to create obstacles, simplicity can quickly feel like an impossible ideal. You're lucky you don't have to work in teams, Diary!

Pinto was one of countless students who either dropped out after failing due to misplaced priorities or, change careered paths after graduating, never fully utilising their degrees—despite ranking highly on the national admissions exam and being class toppers.

I wasn't going to let myself become like those who drifted aimlessly. My goal was simple: get to the finish line. How? By studying relentlessly and making everything else secondary. As classes began, I discovered a passion for human anatomy, which later evolved into an interest in pathology. I spent countless hours at night absorbed in the textbooks next to the bed as Mom slept. While my classmates gushed about how much they loved the smell of rain and damp earth, I despised the rainy seasons. When the monsoon rains came, the ground floor of our building and the nearby streets would flood with sewage water. The stench of faeces would seep into our room on the second floor as I studied. On stormy days, I waded through knee-deep sewage to get to class, holding my study materials in a bag over my head and my shoes in my other hand, trudging slowly through the muck. Any more commentary on that, and I'd start sounding like one of those Asian parents who brag to their children about how they crossed mountains and fought dragons just to get to school.

The long hours I dedicated to my studies quickly paid off. I became one of the top students in my class, staying at school late to learn everything I could and sharing my knowledge with my peers. One day, my girlfriend of that time pointed out a small but noticeable lump on the left side of my neck. "You should get that checked out," she said. I half-heartedly agreed, brushing it off as a simple sprain and returning to our conversation.

A few days later, I was in the pathology lab, peering into a microscope when I suddenly felt two fingers poking at my neck. It was one of my professors. He asked if I had ever experienced chest palpitations, restlessness, excessive sweating, weight fluctuations, or bouts of panic. Taken aback by the precision of his questions, I replied, "Yes, I've had some of those since childhood." He then asked if the lump caused any pain, to which I casually responded that I hardly noticed it until others did.

"You should go downstairs and see one of our colleagues to get this checked out," he said. I was about to dismiss him with an "I'll get to it," as I turned back to my microscope. But he knew me too well. Without a word, he switched off the microscope light and said, firmly, "Now."

The physician performed a needle aspiration biopsy, inserting a fine needle into the swelling on the side of my neck to extract a sample of the tissue inside the swelling. He sent the sample directly to one of my professors, Rashida, to analyse it under the microscope. After class, I nervously walked into her office, where she was already peering through the microscope lens into the slides. Without looking up, she asked, "Whose biopsy is this?"

"Mine, ma'am," I replied quietly.

Rashida glanced at me, her expression shifting from neutral to concerned. "Who are you closest to in your family?" she asked.

"I live with my mother, ma'am. I'm pretty close to her," I said, growing slightly anxious.

"Can you give me her contact details? I'd like to ask her a few questions," she continued.

I was scared, Diary. But I reassured myself that this was probably routine. After all, I hadn't been in the clinic much yet. I scribbled Mom's number on a notepad and handed it over. Rashida nodded, then gestured toward the door. "Thank you. Please come back once your classes are done for the day."

I attended my last class, but my mind was elsewhere. As soon as it ended, I hurried back to her office. Just as I was about to knock, I saw Mom rushing into the pathology lab, her face pale with fear. My heart sank as I knew something was wrong. She walked right past me into Rashida's office, where a few other doctors, including one of the head and neck surgeons, had gathered. I stood frozen outside, watching them talk for about 15 minutes. When the door finally opened, my mother's eyes met mine. She motioned for me to come inside.

Rashida spoke slowly, choosing her words with care. "We found something concerning in your biopsy. Based on the sample, we believe the symptoms you've experienced since childhood may be related to a genetic condition. Your mother told us your grandmother had thyroid cancer, and that family history, combined with your results, leads us to suspect the same diagnosis for you. But we've caught it early, and it's still curable. We just need to act fast and surgically remove the tumour in your neck."

The room fell silent, and I could feel Mom's hand tighten around mine.

"But can't I wait until after I finish my degree? I finally have a handle on my studies, and for the first time in my life, I have a clear goal!" I mumbled, my voice cracking, tears threatening to fall.

Rashida's tone remained firm but compassionate. "You've had isolated symptoms for years, but now it's finally progressed into a tumour." She handed me a small mirror, and for the first time, I truly saw the lump on the left side of my neck, large and ominous. "If you leave it untreated, it could grow larger and potentially damage important blood vessels and nerves. The risks of surgery are low right now, but I can't promise how it will be in a few years."

I knew there was another issue, one that no one wanted to talk about but hung in the air. "How much will it cost?" I asked quietly.

Before Rashida could respond, Mom squeezed my hand tightly, signalling for me to stop. Her silence told me everything I needed to know: she was planning to use up her entire savings on me if she needed to.

Rashida continued, "We can schedule your surgery within two weeks. It's best to let your loved ones know and prepare."

With that, the conversation ended, and preparations began.

The night before the surgery, I sat on the hospital bed, trying to focus on the pre-op procedures. I distracted myself by reading the consent form, smiling as I mentally connected the medications listed with what I had learned in pharmacology that year. It was a small comfort, an attempt to stay grounded amidst the fear and anxiety.

In the corner of the room, I spotted Yamina, Mahima, Shiro, and Rajesh huddled on the extra bed, chatting like they were the best of friends, an odd yet surprisingly cohesive group. Meanwhile, Mohfeez was at my side, quietly helping me with the paperwork. *Nanu* was weeping quietly next to the door, guilt wracking her frail body as she whispered over and over, "If I had been more educated, maybe I would've known how to prevent this, and you wouldn't have to carry my curse."

Yamina interrupted, "Ma, that's not how genetics work. You didn't do this."

Mohfeez, trying to lighten the heavy air, chimed in with a grin, "Ma, if it's your fault, why did it skip a generation? One of us should've had it too, right?" His attempt at humour was well-meaning, but it barely registered.

Then, Mom walked in, Nida following close behind. I hadn't seen her in years. Mom told me she was stepping out for errands earlier, but it was clear she had been arranging something far more important. She headed straight to Mahima and discreetly pulled out several bundles of cash. It was probably everything she had in savings—her life's work spent in an instant for my treatment. Nida, too, handed over several bundles. She didn't have to—there was no familial obligation—but she still did. I couldn't bring myself to ask if they had anything left afterward. The guilt was already too heavy to bear.

I asked Nida, "Why?" She looked at me with a soft smile and replied, "You did the same for us. It's only fair that we stand by you when you need us. Yaad left the country last year to pursue a Master's degree, so I'm here in his place."

I know Yaad took his oath to become a doctor last year. He invited Mom to the ceremony. Mom said watching him on stage, accepting his graduation scroll, was the proudest moment of her life. Even though we hadn't kept in regular touch over the past few years, it warmed my heart to know he had followed Mom's advice and was chasing a collective dream by going for a Master's degree.

As I sat there, Mohfeez nudged me to keep reading the consent form. The risks jumped out at me—permanent damage to my voice box, facial paralysis, possible death. But none of it scared me as much as the thought of what this might cost my mother in her later years.

The nurse had one last thing to say, "Please sign here if you consent to that."

Without a second thought, I signed everything, not even bothering to read the fine print again. The life lessons I usually shared with Yaad now felt hollow. None of them seemed to apply anymore.

That night at 12:00 am, when everyone had left, and it was just Mom, the boys and me. We talked like we used to. For a brief moment, I felt like a child again—laughing, smiling, and soaking in the warmth of our conversation. Every now and then, I caught glimpses of Mom, her smile strained, barely masking the worry etched across her face. As I lay in bed, I let their voices wash over me, drifting in and out of their conversations. I didn't focus on the words; instead, I lost myself in the sound of their voices. Eventually, I slipped into a deep sleep, the last thing I heard was Sammy's voice saying, "See you soon."

A gentle nudge woke me from my sleep. The nurses had come to prep me for surgery. Mohfeez stood beside me, while Yamina comforted Mom who was struggling to hold back her tears. I smiled at them, trying to reassure them that everything would be fine. They smiled back, weakly, through the tears, as I was wheeled away.

Mohfeez stayed close, walking beside my gurney. "I'll be right at the door the whole time," he said, his voice steady. "Don't you worry."

As I was wheeled into the operating room, I noticed a video camera being lowered from the equipment above, its lens focusing on me. A monitor in the corner of the room displayed a copy of what was being recorded. One of the nurses turned to me and asked, "Could you state your name and date of birth for the camera, please?"

I smiled as I recited the details, trying to keep that smile steady even as I watched the anaesthetic needle approach. Within moments, I felt the world around me dissolve into darkness.

Well, you can tell I didn't die from it—after all, I'm still here, writing this. In fact, I started putting it all down while stuck in my post-operative bed, with nothing better to do. I asked Mom to bring me my diary, figuring I might as well document everything before the boys come barging in to see me...and catch me pouring my heart out to you.

Okay so...

I woke up after the surgery to the sound of my neighbour coughing in the next bed. I tried to turn my neck, but it was stiff and immobilised, wrapped in plaster with a drain leading to a bottle beside me, slowly collecting fluid to keep the swelling down. I attempted to sit up, but my body was too weak. Panic surged as I felt something choking me.

"Nurse!" I croaked, relieved to find my voice still intact, albeit broken and unrecognisable.

The nurse quickly approached, understanding my distress. She adjusted the bed to a semi-upright position and placed an oxygen mask over my face, though I couldn't feel it on the left side of my face. I had lost sensation there and could barely speak, but at least I was alive.

Sufi | Entry 7. My angel

DEAR DIARY,

...

After my surgery, I was moved back to my hospital cabin, where Mom, Mohfeez, and Azhar were waiting for me. The swelling had intensified, and the pain was severe. Azhar approached and said, "If my son were here, he'd offer you the finest selection of weed to take the edge off."

Mohfeez chimed in, "You know, medical marijuana is a real thing."

Azhar laughed, "Don't tell my son that. He'll be lighting one up and shouting '*In the name of science!*' at 4:00 am."

I stared at them blankly, trying to process everything, as the surgeons came by shortly afterwards to explain that this was only half the battle. The next step was radiation therapy, something that, at the time, was only available at a government facility across the city.

One month passed, and I was finally fit enough to be discharged from the hospital. Mom and Mohfeez escorted me to *Nanu*'s place first. Her health had deteriorated rapidly, and now, she was consumed with guilt for having 'passed' this illness on to me.

Mohfeez, trying to lighten the mood again, said, "Ma, for the last time, if you passed this on, one of us should have it too, right? It just doesn't *skip* a generation."

That seemed to calm her down, if only for a moment.

Yaad returned to Bangladesh after a few months and stayed at our place for two weeks, which was a welcome surprise. It felt good to see him again after so long, and we spent hours every day catching up on everything that had happened over the four years we hadn't seen each other.

One afternoon, as we played chess, I asked, "So, what exactly happened after you became a doctor?"

Yaad nodded with a smile. "Yeah, I applied for a master's degree by research. Turns out, that's the prerequisite for doing a PhD. I'm not giving up on that dream! The money I had before traveling abroad covered one year's living expenses for a two-year program. You know how difficult it is to make a living as a fresh medical graduate. The grant funding, as I later learned, was only in place to cover one year's tuition. My supervisor told me not to worry and gave me a clear plan: excel in my studies, get the best grades, and apply for the two internal scholarship rounds within the first year. I felt the odds were in my favour and that I'd secure at least one of them."

I interrupted, "And since you're here after almost a year, I'm assuming you got it?"

Yaad hesitated and then said, "It's complicated. I knew there would be challenges, but I was determined to make it work. Along the way, I met people who treated me like family, providing food and supplies while I pursued my goal. I started assisting my supervisor in the clinics, who worked with road traffic accident survivors. He's a unique man who loves controlling the conversation and tells irrelevant stories. But he's also quick to lose patience when interrupted. He'd often snap, 'Get to the point already!'"

I couldn't help but smile at the vivid picture Yaad painted for me.

Yaad chuckled, then added, "My research manager says that my supervisor is a loving father, a good husband, and a genuinely caring person. But let's be honest—no matter how loving a father someone is, if they're difficult to work with, it doesn't make my life any easier. I don't need a loving father at work who will tell me stories; I just need someone to tell me what is required, so that I can get things done and move on with my day."

I laughed. "You should be careful who you share those opinions with. These days, people get offended over just about anything. Anyway, moving on—what was your living arrangement like?"

Yaad smiled. "I stayed in a shared dorm room, working late into the night with only the glow of my computer screen lighting up the dark space while my roommate snored on the bed across the room. He was obsessed with cooking biryani and indulged in it almost every day. I used to tease him, half-jokingly asking, 'How do you not have a heart attack every week?' Meanwhile, I cooked only once a month, storing my meals—mostly vegetables and rice—in the fridge and eating them bit by bit. By the end of the month, the food would often turn white with mould, so I'd douse it in Caesar salad dressing to mask the taste. For me, food is nothing more than fuel."

I wrinkled my nose. "That's unhealthy and disgusting, Yaad."

He ignored my comment entirely and carried on. "My supervisor's advice was simple: in academia, peer-reviewed publications are the currency for scholarships. He told me that getting two publications in my first year would make a strong case. The first internal scholarship round was just three months away, and that became my timer."

I interjected, "So you had plenty of time!"

Yaad shook his head. "It doesn't work that way. Research and publishing take time—between conducting studies, literature reviews, and the agonisingly slow peer review process. But I dove in headfirst, working 12-hour days. Within those three months, I completed two pilot projects and submitted them to journals. While waiting for peer reviews, I filled out my scholarship application, providing proof of submission, even though I knew the review process was beyond my control."

He moved a chess piece and continued. "I didn't stop there. I stayed active in the lab and clinics, starting more research to strengthen my case for the scholarship interview. When the day finally came, I sat before three assessors. They glanced over my application and said, 'We would've liked to see some publications. Right now, your research profile seems weak.' I quickly replied, 'But I've done the research; the publications will come in due time.' One of them said, 'Publications remain to be seen. You should apply again.' And just like that, I was declined."

As I countered his moves on the chessboard, I replied, "That's tough, man. Funny, though, because no one in the real-world cares how many papers you've published. So, what did you do?"

Yaad's focus was split between the game and his story. "Consistency is key," he said. "I took their feedback seriously and doubled down on my efforts, aiming for the next round five months later. My days stretched to 16-hour sessions of study and research. I churned out paper after paper. By the time the second round approached in five months, I had four published papers and research that could rival a PhD student's. Feeling more confident, I filled out another application and was called in for an interview—same group of assessors."

I grinned. "You showed them! Let me guess—you got the scholarship?"

Yaad smirked and moved his knight into an aggressive position. "I wish. At the interview, one of the assessors said, 'You've worked hard since we last met. Four papers—that's impressive!' But then another assessor pulled out this thick file and said, 'The previous applicant has 40 publications in his portfolio.'"

I raised an eyebrow. "Forty? Were those all published at your university?"

He nodded grimly. "I asked the same thing. They replied, 'No, he just joined. Most of his publications were from before. Yaad, we admire your efforts, but we're inclined to award the scholarship to the other applicant. He has a stronger academic track record.' And just like that, I was declined again."

I didn't know what to say as I moved my rook, buying time to process his story.

Yaad let out a frustrated sigh. "The successful applicant had fifteen years of academic experience, while I'd only been at it for ten months.

Yet we were judged on the same scale, with no consideration for our vastly different career stages."

He moved his queen dangerously close to my king. His queen was protected only by his knight, positioned to check me if I dared take his queen. I frowned at the board, realising my only option was to retreat. This game was heading toward a predictable end, but I couldn't help admiring the way Yaad had set up his victory.

Yaad moved his Bishop to align it with my king. My king was cornered, boxed in by his knight and queen. Checkmate!

Yaad continued, "It felt unfair, but it taught me that only results matter. No one cares about the effort you put in unless your results outshine everyone else's. Effort is assumed; success is what gets acknowledged."

Truer words have never been spoken!

Yaad continued, "I refused to let the assessors' rejection define my worth. I needed to show them—and myself—that I was just as capable as someone with fifteen years in academia. Actions speak louder than words, right? But what I didn't realise was that I was slowly driving myself into a state of cold, emotionless burnout. In the process, I lost the ability to appreciate the small joys that once made life meaningful."

I raised an eyebrow and commented, "But you don't seem burnt out to me now."

He smiled faintly. "That's because things changed for the better one day. Our research team was called into the clinic to meet a young boy, about nine years old, who walked in with his father. The boy was missing his left eye. His father explained that his son had lost it at age four and was now being relentlessly bullied at school. The boy had begged his father to 'make him look normal again.' After searching everywhere, they found our clinic. The moment I saw the boy, he looked familiar—too familiar. Or maybe it was his story. I started seeing myself in him."

A lump formed in my throat, and a tear rolled down my cheek. I could see Sammy in the child Yaad described, although he didn't know it. Diary, I never told Yaad about the bullying Sammy endured or that she committed suicide. If he knew how I failed to protect her, I feared he'd lose faith in me. Mom told him Sammy passed away in her sleep when we were very young, and I ran with it.

Yaad's voice softened as he continued, "My supervisor was moved by the boy's story and said, 'Let's help him.' The challenge was immense. After so many years without an eye, the muscles around his socket had contracted, making it nearly impossible to create a prosthetic that would stay in place. But my supervisor wouldn't let it go. My task was to surgically carve out space in the socket, making room for something to fit, while our prosthetics team burned the midnight oil in the lab, testing out new designs."

I was captivated as I urged him to continue. "What happened next?"

"Our team got to work," Yaad said, his eyes gleaming with emotion. "The boy came in every day, and I kept trying different methods. Each attempt failed—the prosthetic would inevitably fall out. But after countless trials and errors, we finally created a prosthesis that stayed in place. The nurse led the boy to the mirror, and he carefully put it on."

I nodded, asking him to continue.

Yaad continued, "He stared at his reflection for a moment, then turned to us with the biggest, most genuine smile I've ever seen. In that instant, all the bitterness I'd nurtured over the years seemed to fade away, leaving behind a glimmer of hope I hadn't felt in ages. I smiled back. For the first time, I truly fell in love with research—not as a means to get ahead but as a way to make a real difference in people's lives."

I sat in silence, moved by his story. Finally, I asked, "And now?"

Yaad leaned back in his chair as he stared at the chess board and the game he won. "Now I realise there's more to life than grinding non-stop for success that others might withhold based on subjective standards. Sure, I'll go back and finish my degree. I even got a research assistantship before I came to see you. The job technically pays the same as a scholarship. But what felt more important was I wanted to come back and be with the people who actually mattered."

Yaad opened up about everything wrong with academia and the common misconception that migrating overseas guarantees easy jobs. He explained that these so-called "easy" jobs are typically reserved for locals, while immigrants are left with the roles that locals refuse to take. Yet, despite this, locals don't hesitate to blame immigrants for "taking their jobs!" He also pointed out how Western governments entice people with promises of lucrative opportunities, only to pull the rug out by changing clauses to the immigrants' visas when it suits the governing body's agenda. While some call it "constantly adapting," Yaad bluntly referred to it as a "lack of foresight." I wouldn't know much beyond what I've seen on the news and Yaad's stories since I've never been to another country myself—though I'd love to visit someday! Who knows? Maybe I'll even end up following Yaad wherever he goes... like a creepy stalker!

It felt good to finally reconnect with Yaad after all these years. As he left, a part of me sensed that this might be the last time we'd cross paths. But in that moment, I couldn't help but feel an overwhelming pride in the person he had become.

A month later, I checked myself in for radiation therapy at the only government-authorised radiation-administering hospital in the country: a dilapidated four-story relic from the 1980s. The building looked like it had been awarded to a contractor on some shady, politically-influenced tender—crumbling, barely maintained, much like the way my life felt at the time.

The treatment plan was simple: I'd take a radioactive iodine tablet on the first day that would target and gradually destroy my cancer cells while I remain confined to a room for 14 days as the radiation from the tablet inside my body diminished to a safe level. Mom and I arrived a day early, standing outside the facility's gates. The building's third and fourth floors were connected by a wide, open balcony, giving a stark view of the neglected structure. We rang the bell, and a short man in his late forties opened the gate. He wore a red shirt, black pants, and sandals. His long moustache extended into his sideburns, and his sunken eyes and blemished skin bore the toll of hard years. He grinned, revealing decayed teeth.

"I am Surya! I look after the facility!" he said, smiling awkwardly.

"Just you? Or your entire team?" I asked, half-joking, trying to gauge the state of this place.

"There was another woman here who worked full-time with me a while back—a nurse," Surya began, pausing to gauge whether I was paying attention.

I nodded to reassure him. "What happened to her?" I asked.

Surya hesitated before continuing, "Oh, one morning she informed us she was pregnant..." He trailed off, leaving his sentence dangling awkwardly.

I tried to fill the silence. "So, she's on maternity leave?"

Surya smirked. "No, she was let go. Not every line of work affords the luxury of extended holidays."

"Let go because she was pregnant?" I pressed.

"Not exactly," Surya clarified. "She started refusing to clean patient rooms—something clearly outlined in her job description—and then asked to work fewer hours all of a sudden because 'radiation is not good for the baby!' Look, pregnancy is a choice, not a disease. She chose to keep the baby, which is fine, but it doesn't mean management will give her special treatment when her choices put more work on the rest of us."

"Wouldn't it have been better to keep her on part-time, even at reduced pay? It seems like something is better than nothing, especially now when you're short-staffed," I countered.

"The bosses did offer her part-time work," Surya replied, then mimicking the nurse's voice in a mocking tone, he continued. "'No, please, I can't take part-time. This full-time job is all we have, and I don't know how we'll pay the bills otherwise!'" He chuckled and continued, "For her circumstances, getting an abortion would probably have been better for her financial well-being, but who am I to say that, right?"

Surya was a blunt man, Diary. With the global pro-life and pro-choice movements sparking heated debates, his views would undoubtedly ignite controversy. Yet, his perspective touched on a bitter reality—financial instability often strains marriages, sometimes to their breaking point. Is it fair to bring a child into a life of hardship, risking a future as a single parent struggling to make ends meet? Not every child raised under difficult circumstances grows up to become Eminem or, for that matter, an academic like Yaad!

It's true that circumstances can improve over time. Many parents hope their financial situation will change for the better, seizing the opportunity when it arises, even if it means taking a leap of faith. But the decision to continue or terminate a pregnancy is deeply personal. Parents rarely welcome unsolicited commentary, even from their accountant or family doctor. They expect empathy and support, especially from employers and colleagues. In Western countries where workforce shortages prevail, such expectations and accommodations might be feasible. But in places like Bangladesh, where skilled labour is abundant and language barriers are non-existent, the math seems different to me.

After a moment of reflection, I asked, "So you're the only full-time attendant now?"

Surya laughed bitterly. "Management says I'm doing just fine on my own and doesn't see the point of hiring anyone else. We've got other nurses, sure, but they're all 'on-call' casual staff. They only show up for emergencies."

He shrugged, his tone casual, but his words hinted at a deeper frustration as the final joke was on him.

"I'm the one who cleans the rooms and looks after the guests," Surya added, leading us toward a heavy security gate inside the ground floor.

He turned to Mom and said, "I'm sorry, ma'am, no visitors beyond this point. If you have anything for him to take upstairs, now's the time. I can also bring up anything else you think of later in the mornings."

Mom handed me bedsheets, a change of clothes, my medications, some of my textbooks, and some money. When we were done, Surya unlocked the gate, revealing a dark, unlit staircase. He smiled again and turned to Mom. "Could you be a dear and wait here? I'll take your son up and come back to lock up and leave with you."

"Locked up?" I asked, alarmed.

Surya chuckled, "Just policy. Many patients, especially from rural Bangladesh, don't understand the dangers of residual radiation to their loved ones. They try to leave after a day or two, so we keep things secure."

I noticed something odd and couldn't help but point it out. "But... you're not wearing any protective gear."

Surya shrugged with a casual grin, "Only the doctors wear those suits when they come to give the medicine. I've been here twenty years, and they've never given me anything like that. So, it must be okay!"

I knew it wasn't. His words stung with the reality of neglect—this was just one of many cost-cutting measures, sacrifices for the sake of keeping treatment affordable for the poorest. As if to say, like some war general, "Sacrifice one life to save many."

As we moved up to the third floor, Surya gestured "And here we are," guiding me into a dim corridor, the lone overhead light barely illuminating the space. The corridor divided the rooms on either side, and all the rooms shared access to a surrounding balcony. If it weren't for the faint afternoon light seeping through the open balcony doors, I wouldn't have been able to see much at all.

He ushered me into what would be my room for the next 14 days—a small but cozy space with a high-legged hospital bed, leaving enough room beneath it to stow my suitcase. A single chair sat in the corner, and a modern sliding glass door, frosted for privacy, led to the balcony. The sliding balcony door had no lock and looked out of place amidst the building's aging architecture, likely a recent addition. The building had been operational for decades, with minimal renovations—just enough to keep it functional, like putting a band-aid on a wound too big to heal properly.

"You're lucky," Surya remarked with a grin. "One of the only two rooms with direct access to the balcony. All the others only have windows. So, in a way, you won't be completely isolated. You can walk around the balcony whenever you like!"

I smiled awkwardly. "Where is everyone else?"

"There was an old woman who's been here with us for the past month. She left this morning and said she might come back tomorrow. The rest will be brought in by bus tomorrow morning."

Picking up on his comment, I asked, "Wait, the old woman left and will come back tomorrow? Why was she allowed to leave?"

Surya nodded. "Her therapy ended a while ago. No one came to pick her up, so she paid extra to stay for a few more days until she could reach her family in the village."

I raised an eyebrow. "What if she finishes whatever she left for by tonight?"

He shrugged. "Then she'll have to spend the night on the streets. I'll be locking up the premises behind me."

Glancing at my phone as I fidgeted with it. "Do you have any plans for what you'll do all alone these next 14 days?"

I shrugged. "I'll study and keep in touch with my family. Seems like a good time to make up for the time I've lost getting caught up in life."

he said, "Great choice!" he said, grinning again. "Too bad you don't have a TV like your neighbours, but that room's got two beds and only one channel, so you're not missing much!"

His strange enthusiasm made me uneasy, but I thanked him anyway. He then led me to the shared bathroom at the end of the corridor. Flicking on the light, he revealed a cramped, run-down space: the sink was cracked, and the showerhead was missing, but there was a functioning toilet—thankfully not a pan latrine like in many older homes where you had to squat down to do your business. I sighed in quiet relief.

After showing me around, Surya handed me a scrap of paper with his number scrawled on it. "I live nearby, so don't hesitate to call if you need anything. I'll take my leave now while you settle in."

As he left, I watched him lock the staircase gate behind him. It struck me as odd. I quickly walked out to the balcony and leaned over the metal railing. From above, I saw my mother and Surya exchange a few words before he locked the main gate and they went their separate ways.

Back inside, the fading sunlight dimmed the room further, so I flicked on the fluorescent light. That's when I noticed scrawled in what looked like red nail polish on one of the walls were the words, *"My Angel."*

It felt like something straight out of a horror movie.

I spread a queen-sized bedsheet over the small bed, the fabric draping all the way to the floor even after I'd tucked it in. With my room somewhat in order, I grabbed my toiletries and headed to the bathroom. The corridor was dimly lit, just enough to guide my way, as the sounds of the empty building echoed around me.

After finishing in the bathroom, I turned off the lights and followed the faint glow seeping from my room to find my way back. The air was humid, so I switched on the ceiling fan and collapsed onto the bed, staring blankly as the blades spun in their slow, circular rhythm. That's when Mohfeez called.

"Sufi, how are you?" he asked, trying to sound upbeat.

I don't know what came over me, but I broke down. Tears flooded out as I told him everything—how hard I had tried to keep things together, how no matter what I did, it always felt like my sanity was slipping beyond my control. I was likely having a full-on breakdown, and he was the only person I felt safe enough to let see it.

He stayed quiet, listening patiently until I was done. After a long pause, he finally spoke, his voice calm but serious. "We're all counting on you to make something of yourself. *Nanu* is especially counting on you, and she doesn't have much time left. Even I'm counting on you," he added with a wry chuckle, "though I might not be far behind her."

Through my sobbing, I tried to brush off his attempt at humour. "Yeah, I know. It's not generational, because none of you have it."

There was a heavy silence before he replied, his tone more sombre. "Who said it's not generational? You and *Nanu* were suffering enough, and she kept blaming herself, convinced she passed this curse onto you. What kind of son would I be if I added to that burden by telling her I was diagnosed a few months ago too?"

My crying stopped in an instant, replaced by disbelief. "What did you just say?"

"Yes," he repeated quietly. "I was diagnosed too, the same as *Nanu*. But mine spread to the lungs. No amount of surgery will help there. The doctors say chemo and radiation might buy me some time, but that's all."

"I'm so sorry," I whispered, struggling to find words. "But why are you telling me this now?"

He sighed. "Because yours hasn't spread. It's still early, and you have time. You are all your mother has left, Sufi. She's spent everything—her life's savings—on your education and your treatment. You need to stay strong, for her."

I nodded, barely able to speak. "I understand."

"Good," he said gently. "But let's keep this between us for now. We may not have much, but we all love you. Don't ever think you're alone."

I agreed, and after a quiet goodbye, I hung up.

Still shaken, I reached for my phone again to call my mother, but just then, messages popped up from my mischievous cousin Nessa asking how I was doing. Trying to recover from my conversation with Mohfeez, I decided to reply. I joked about the creepy *'My Angel'* message scrawled on my wall, and she immediately went with it, spinning absurd, spooky scenarios about what might happen in the night. It was exactly what I needed—a light-hearted distraction. We laughed and chatted for hours, the familiar banter easing some of my tension.

By the time we said goodnight, it was nearly midnight. I turned off the lights and tucked myself into bed, the room now dark except for the faint moonlight filtering through the balcony door. Just as I was about to drift off, I heard a flick—like a switch being turned on—in the corridor outside.

Too tired and drained from my daily medication, I ignored it, sinking further into the bed as sleep finally took over.

I woke to the sound of rumbling and commotion. Groggy, I checked my phone—6:00 am. I opened my door to find Surya leading a group of twelve individuals, each likely farmers or fishermen from rural Bangladesh, all victims of a cruel disease too expensive to treat. He moved quickly, assigning people to rooms. A boy, no more than eight years old, was placed in the room to my left, and two elderly women in the room to my right. As Surya passed, I asked, "What's the boy's condition?"

Surya sighed, a heaviness in his voice. "Isn't it heartbreaking? Late-stage liver cancer, at such a young age. He just finished radiotherapy and needs to stay here for a few days of isolation." Then, almost as if to lighten the mood, he added cheerfully, "Good morning, though! Look at all your new neighbours!" He continued down the hall, ushering everyone into their rooms, and the once-empty floor quickly came to life.

Next door, the women turned on the TV, laughing and chatting in their regional dialects. The contrast between their joy and the sorrow hanging over the boy's room left mixed feelings in me. Curious about the others, I stepped onto the balcony, starting a slow walk around, passing the windows of each room. I saw people unpacking their small pouches of belongings, their faces etched with exhaustion and worry. When I reached one window, a young woman stood by the bars, her face streaked with tears.

She noticed me and asked, "How do you get to the balcony? I'd like to see my daughter."

I hesitated. "I'm sorry, only two rooms have doors to the balcony."

Her voice cracked. "You're lucky. Could you please check if my husband and daughter are still downstairs?"

I leaned over the railing and spotted a man standing by the curb, cradling an infant, a cloth pouch at his feet. His eyes met mine, pleading silently. I returned to the woman and told her they were still there. She broke down, her words spilling out through sobs. "I told him not to sell everything for my treatment. He wouldn't listen. What's going to happen to our daughter now?"

I fumbled for something to say. "I'm sorry... What happened?"

She wiped her tears and explained, "I have cancer. The doctors said my treatment was expensive, and something only the city could provide. We're simple farmers. My husband sold the little land we had. He promised we'd figure it out after I got better... but I know he was just saying that to make me feel better"

I mumbled another apology, feeling utterly helpless, and walked away. As I passed the boy's room, I noticed him curled up on the floor, writhing in pain. My heart raced. I rushed back to my room, grabbed my phone, and called Surya. Thankfully, he was downstairs with an on-call nurse, and they hurried to help. They carried the boy to the second floor, where a doctor was called in. I stood silently at my doorway, watching it all unfold.

Afterwards, I sat on my bed and pulled out the biscuits Mom had packed for breakfast. I nibbled on them slowly, knowing I had to keep it light before my radiation treatment. An hour later, two elderly doctors arrived, dressed in hazmat suits, carrying a heavy, sealed container. One of them asked me to open my mouth as he carefully slid a small capsule from the container into my throat.

"Will the others here get the same medication?" I asked.

He smiled kindly. "No, you're the only one receiving an oral radiation tablet this session. The others have already undergone different treatments and are here for just a few days until it's safe for them to return. If we don't keep them isolated, they'll likely return to work before the radiation has worn off, putting others at risk."

I nodded, recalling Surya's words earlier.

The treatment itself felt uneventful, but the effects soon kicked in. A wave of fever hit me, and I passed out for nearly ten hours.

When I woke, the sound of an infant crying reached me. It was distant, coming from outside. The fever had broken, so I stepped out onto the balcony to find the source. Below, the farmer sat on the curbside, cradling his crying infant. The streets had quieted as dusk approached, and the sound echoed more clearly.

I turned to the window of the woman's room. She was crying too. As I approached, she murmured, "She's probably hungry. What do I do?"

There was nothing I could offer. Walking further along the balcony. I saw a frail elderly woman, perhaps in her seventies, standing alone, gazing out at the streets below. She occupied the other room with a balcony door. Hearing my footsteps, she turned and asked, "How many days are you in for?"

It felt like a prison sentence the way she phrased it. "Fourteen days," I replied. "And you?"

"I'm not sure," she said flatly, her voice weak and worn down by the side effects of the treatment. "Whenever someone comes to pick me up."

This must be the old woman Surya had told me about. I hesitated before asking, "Have you tried calling them?"

"Yes," she sighed. "But they've stopped answering my calls."

"Don't you know where your village is? Maybe you could just leave and take a bus?"

"I tried," she said, sounding defeated. "I went to the post office, described my hometown as best I could, hoping someone would recognise the address and help me get there. But I've been losing my memory since my illness, and my descriptions haven't been enough. I've even been to the police station and the post office multiple times, even yesterday. Still no luck."

I paused, unsure if I wanted to ask, but I did anyway. "How long do you think you can keep this up?"

She gave a tired smile. "I've given Surya the last of the money I brought with me to stay here a bit longer. After that... I don't know."

The woman likely had a brain tumour or metastasis that was impairing her cognitive function. Every day, I saw her standing on the balcony, gazing at the streets with a hopeful look. She had probably been doing this for as long as she'd been here, waiting for someone who might never come.

It wasn't the first time I'd heard something like this. Many poorer families, unable to afford the rising costs of treatment, would abandon their elderly halfway through. It was a heartbreaking reality, often unnoticed unless it made the news. Recently, hear the story about a visually impaired mother, also suffering from partial hearing loss, who was left at a bus stand by her family. She didn't realise what was happening until her son had disappeared, and then she began to cry. The abandonment felt cruel, but in many cases, families were trapped between poverty and impossible healthcare costs.

In Bangladesh, there is no legal obligation to care for elderly family members, which leaves many struggling with the moral dilemma of what to do when old age homes are unaffordable, and the costs of care for terminal illnesses or chronic diseases are overwhelming.

In the span of an hour, I had seen two kinds of people: those who would bankrupt themselves to care for their loved ones, and those who, out of sheer desperation, felt they had no choice but to let them go. Both situations were tragic, born out of love and the limits of what people could bear.

I felt that same helplessness from earlier take over me. "I'm sorry," I whispered, offering no more than empty words before retreating back to my room.

I took out some dry cake from my bag and ate it for dinner, reflecting on the lives of those around me. How hard their struggles were, and how blessed I was, even in the midst of my own difficulties. That led me to an important life lesson: Someone always has it worse.

There will always be someone who has it harder than you. It's better to try and make the most of the privileges that you're given rather than dwell on the setbacks.

As I ate, a sudden wave of fever and nausea took over, pulling me into an uneasy sleep. The following morning, I woke to heavy commotion in the narrow lobby. As I peeked out, I saw Surya and another nurse wheeling a stretcher past my door, a small body bag on top. The boy with liver cancer had passed away during the night.

I stood there for a moment, not knowing how to process it. Life and death felt so close, yet so distant at the same time. Needing a distraction, I joined the queue for the bathroom. It was a long wait, and while standing in line, I saw two other patients leaving with Surya.

As the days went by, one by one, the rooms emptied out, until there were only four of us left by the ninth day. Every day, I would see the old woman stand on the balcony from sunrise to sunset looking down at the streets, hoping someone would come and take her home.

On the nineth morning, I heard the familiar sound of an infant crying outside, just as before. But this time, the hurried footsteps in the corridor caught my attention. I peeked out again, just in time to see the young woman rushing downstairs to reunite with her husband and child. She had been discharged. But to what life? They had sold everything for her treatment—what kind of future could they possibly rebuild now?

Later that same morning, the police arrived to escort the old woman out. Her privilege to stay was up. But even they seemed uncertain of where to send her, and even if they're successful, the fate she'd face—whether abandoned again or left to fend for herself—was as unclear to them as it was to her.

By that night, there were only two of us left—me and one of the older women next door. Around 11:00 pm, I was on the phone with Nida, catching up on the usual family drama. She was cheerful, but mid-conversation, I heard her snap at someone in the background, calling out Kaushal's name in the same sharp tone our father used to use.

"Careful, you sound just like him!" I teased.

She shot back, frustrated, "I gave him one job and he can't even do that right!"

I laughed, thinking it was the typical back-and-forth between husband and wife. As we chatted, I could have sworn I heard footsteps on the balcony outside my room—strange, since the only other room with access to the balcony was now empty. Curious and a little uneasy, I told Nida I'd call her back and went to investigate.

I slid open the door and peeked out—nothing. *"My mind must be playing tricks on me again,"* I thought, trying to shake off the unease. I decided to brush my teeth and call it a night. I flipped off the ceiling fan, grabbed my toothbrush and phone, and headed to the bathroom, using my phone's flashlight to navigate the dim hallway.

As I brushed my teeth, the silence was broken by faint thudding sounds, as if someone—or something—was running around on the balcony. A chill ran down my spine, but I tried to brush it off as nerves. When I returned to my room, everything seemed normal, except for one thing—the stand beside my bed, used for hanging infusion bags, was slowly revolving very slowly, as if a breeze was pushing it. It was odd—especially since the ceiling fan was off. The wind howled outside, its fierce gusts likely bleeding into the room just enough to cause that subtle movement. I couldn't shake the feeling that something was amiss.

I stared at it for a moment, but rational explanations won over curiosity. I set my phone down and climbed into bed, telling myself it was nothing.

That night, at 3:00 am, amidst a thunderstorm I woke to the sound of a baby crying—the same cry I'd heard before, the one from the young farmer's child. But they had left two days ago. As I listened closer, the crying seemed to come not from the street below, but from the balcony right outside my room. It grew louder, turning from soft whimpers into blood-curdling shrieks.

My heart raced, but I kept repeating to myself, "It's just my mind playing tricks. This isn't real." Over and over, like a mantra, until the words became a lullaby that somehow, amidst the fear, lulled me back to sleep.

On the twelfth day, I woke up feeling utterly drained, as if I hadn't slept at all. My eyes struggled to adjust, and I noticed the sliding door to the balcony was partially open. I rushed over to check it. It had no locks, so I figured I might have left it slightly ajar, or maybe the wind had pushed it open, just like it had played tricks on me before, mimicking the sound of a child's cry.

Still shaken, I left for the bathroom. As I brushed my teeth, I heard a door creak open down the hallway. With the toothbrush still in my mouth, I cracked the bathroom door to peek out. The remaining lady from the room with the TV next to mine was leaving, guided by

Surya. Oddly, this time, he didn't lock the gate to our floor behind him. I sighed, realising I'd be all alone for the next two days.

Just as I was about to close the bathroom door, something caught my eye in the unoccupied room next to the bathroom. The door was wide open, and on the walls were dried bloodstains, splattered in a disturbing pattern from a central point of impact. I finished brushing and walked inside the room to take a closer look. The stains seemed old, but their presence was unnerving.

I stepped back into the hallway and found Surya had come back upstairs to lock the gate. He had left a package at my door—likely food from my mother. I called out to him, "Surya, did anything happen in that room? An accident, maybe?" I pointed to the room near the bathroom.

Surya stared at it for a moment, as if trying to recall. "All sorts of crazy things happen when people are in isolation. There was one guy who started bashing his head against the wall because of the pain. We found him in the morning, pretty beat up. Had to patch him up."

I hesitated before asking, "Was there a lot of blood?"

Surya shrugged casually. "Every room has seen something over the past two decades. There was even a suicide in one of them, but I can't remember which one," he said with a grin before walking away.

I stood there, stunned by how casually he spoke about it. Shaken but trying to brush it off, I went back to my room and attempted to catch up on some studies. By evening, exhaustion crept in, and I decided to turn off the lights and lie down.

Around 11:00 pm, as I was tossing and turning in bed, my heart skipped a beat. A silhouette appeared on the other side of the frosted glass door leading to the balcony. For a brief moment, it just stood there. I rubbed my eyes, trying to make sense of what I was seeing. The figure seemed to stare at the glass for nearly a minute before slowly turning and walking away.

Disturbed, I forced myself to check. I opened the door to the balcony, but there was no one there. I was the only person on the entire floor—possibly in the whole building. Feeling uneasy, I closed the balcony door and crawled back into bed.

At 1:45 am, I started hearing music, not from the street below, but from the walls around me. It was faint, interrupted by occasional commentary, like a radio or TV show. My heart raced as I realised the sound was coming from the room next to mine, where no one had been staying. I got out of bed and cautiously approached the window to check. Sure enough, the TV in the next room was on, flickering in the dark, but the room was empty.

I told myself it had to be a faulty TV turning on by itself, but deep down, a part of me feared something more sinister. I hurried back to my room, my mind racing. Fear is a funny thing—it can make your body react in unexpected ways. In my case, it gave me the sudden urge to rush to the bathroom. As I got out of the bathroom after doing what I needed to do, I noticed the door to the room next to the bathroom, the one with the bloodstains, was now closed. I distinctly remembered seeing it wide open earlier. I tried the knob—it was locked from the inside.

My heart began to pound in my chest. I ran back to my room, locked the door, and sat on a chair by the balcony door, trying to calm myself. That's when I heard it—the sound of the locked door slowly creaking open. In the silence of the night, every sound was magnified. I could hear footsteps coming closer to my room. I held my breath, trying to stay as quiet as possible, as though doing so would deter someone who was standing right outside from coming in.

Then, the knob on my door began to wiggle, but the door didn't open—it was locked. My heart raced faster. The knob twisted again, and that's when I lost it. I screamed, "Who's there?!"

Suddenly, everything went still. The cold air in the room seemed to drop a few degrees, and a heavy silence filled the space. I couldn't stay locked inside, paralysed by fear, so I pulled the infusion stand out from the bed post like a weapon and slowly walked out onto the balcony. I felt safer in the open, away from the claustrophobic walls.

As I cautiously circled the balcony, the moonlight revealed a chilling sight. In the room where I had first spoken to the young farmer's wife, a shadowy figure sat motionless on the bed. The light was just bright enough for me to know someone was there, yet the darkness was so thick that I couldn't make out most of the facial features. Its lifeless eyes stared back at me through the metal grill, frozen in time, as if it had been waiting for me all along.

All my defences crumbled as I bolted back into my room, frantically jamming the sliding door with a chair wedged against the wall in a futile attempt to keep it shut. Clutching the infusion stand, I climbed onto the bed, trembling, mumbling to myself. My eyes fixated on the words "My Angel" scrawled across the wall. A chilling thought crept into me—it wasn't nail polish. It was likely blood.

The last thing I remembered before drifting into a fitful sleep was the sound of the water tap in the bathroom. It turned on by itself, then shut off just as abruptly.

When I awoke a few hours later, around 6:00 am, I was still curled up in the corner. To my horror, the balcony door was wide open. As I swung my legs off the bed, I stumbled over my suitcase, which had been pulled out from under the bed, even though I distinctly remembered stowing it away. Someone had been in my room while I slept. My belongings had been rifled through.

I glanced around, and the infusion stand, which had been in my hands, was now missing. It wasn't on the bedpost either. My heart pounded as I fumbled for my phone and called Mom, begging her to come and get me out immediately. Within an hour, she arrived, and got a nurse to unlock the door, letting me out. The nurse said Surya was on his leave.

As I hastily packed my belongings, I noticed the money my mother had given me at check-in was missing. Ignoring it, I threw everything into my bags and rushed out. As I loaded my suitcase onto a rickshaw, I suddenly remembered that I had left the bedsheet and pillow cover behind. Mom was puzzled by my sense of urgency and asked what had me so spooked.

As the rickshaw pulled away, I turned back to look at the building one last time. My blood ran cold. There, on the balcony, stood Surya, holding the infusion stand in his hands, watching me leave.

That's when it all clicked. Surya hadn't just slipped into my room the night before—he had *never left.* He'd been likely hiding under my bed, waiting for the right moment to rob me on his day off. Think about the countless vulnerable patients—many from poor, rural areas—who were likely robbed in the same way. People like Surya preyed on the weak, supplementing their miserable wages by taking advantage of those too scared or sick to fight back. They worked in dangerous, thankless conditions, but their choices to exploit others added another layer of injustice.

In the days that followed, I filed a formal complaint. The investigation revealed that Surya had likely been running this scam for quite some time, comfortably living in the isolation ward and discreetly robbing patients without anyone noticing. The victims, often too frightened or powerless to speak up, feared that reporting the theft would lead to delays in their treatment or even worse—vindictive retaliation. In many similar cases across the country, clinic assistants, receptionists, and caretakers like Surya accept bribes to expedite certain patients' appointments, exploiting their desperation for medical care—often without the doctors' knowledge.

By the time the investigation got underway, someone had likely tipped Surya off, who had vanished without a trace, and management dropped the case scrambling to hire a new caretaker. Yet the memory of that night, and the unnerving thought that he had been lurking so close to me for hours, lingered long after I'd left that place. Little did I know, that wouldn't be the last time I'd find myself in that place.

Despite everything that had happened at the isolation ward, I returned feeling hopeful—grateful for the life I still had. But at the dental school, things were far from easy. I had fallen behind drastically, and with missed assessments and attendance issues, I was at serious risk of failing the year. My girlfriend at the time, along with a few close friends, rallied around me, helping me catch up on my studies, walking me through the material I'd missed. Faculty members, too, went out of their way, staying after hours to give me reassessments, ensuring I had a chance to catch up. I still ended up failing a year. Bitterness seeped in as I watched everyone around me move forward in life and secure lucrative training and career opportunities while I remained stuck, despite all my efforts. I became unjustly resentful toward my girlfriend, blaming her for my hardships, and that relationship eventually crumbled under the weight of my own insecurities.

Failing meant more than just falling behind; it shattered my chances of contending for distinctions. Even worse, my grades for the remainder of dental school would be capped at a pass, severely jeopardising my ability to apply for scholarships to study abroad. Mom's passion for higher education and Yaad's drive had finally influenced me to see that anyone is capable of doing a PhD if they set their mind to it, and I was beginning to grasp my studies more firmly. Now, I too had *miles to go before I slept*!

While it's true that when you pursue something you love, you never work a day in your life, the same can be said for studying a subject you are passionate about. I loved dentistry—every aspect of it. Everyone at the dental school knew this, including the faculty, who recognised my potential. They understood my circumstances and actively encouraged my friends to help me with assignments, even though, in a stricter, more Western academic setting, this might have been seen as academic collusion.

For the next two years, I fought through. I took two assessments every day after hours while attending classes and clinics during the day.

The side effects of the medication were brutal—constant headaches made focusing on anything unbearable at times—but I pushed through, driven by the simple fact that life had given me a second chance.

Outside of school, I'd see Mohfeez slowly lose more weight, likely because of the advanced stage of his undisclosed cancer. This was a secret I did not want to keep, but had no choice. Mom, meanwhile, started working two jobs to rebuild her savings, and I didn't see her as much as I used to.

life never went back to what it once was. *Nanu* passed away a few months later, as cancer ravaged her brain. I was the one to lower her into her grave. A year later, Mohfeez became bedridden, his body wasting away as his own cancer was finally revealed to everyone. He too passed, and I lowered him into his grave as well.

I eventually graduated and became a dentist. As I had predicted, failing a year meant my grades slipped to an average level, effectively closing the door on any scholarship opportunities that I had to study abroad. After facing multiple rejections, it became clear that a scholarship was unattainable. I decided to work and tutor, saving every penny that I could diligently to apply for an affordable degree in an Asian country like Yaad. Now a full fee-paying student, I thought, *"What could go wrong?"*

My first visa application was rejected. The foreign authorities cited health requirements, deeming my cancer a potential burden on their healthcare system. It wasn't an unreasonable concern—much of the Western world, and the Middle East also enforce strict health screenings, welcoming only those who meet their rigorous standards of fitness. For someone like me who was in the midst of battling an invisible struggle, the decision to remain honest and disclose a health condition felt like an impossible gamble.

As an immigrant chasing a better life, revealing one's vulnerabilities isn't always a viable option. It's a cruel paradox where we are often left to choose the lesser of two evils, as Yaad puts it: disclosing a disease could mean your dreams will end abruptly and extinguish a future before it even begins. Concealing it, however, means carrying the weight of the medical condition, silently coexisting with an unwelcome truth in a foreign land, perhaps forever. The choice feels less like a decision and more like an ultimatum—survival versus honesty.

But despite countless appeals and attempts to demonstrate my qualifications—hoping my skills would outweigh a disease I never chose—I was unsuccessful. I was finally granted entry only after I convinced a senior colleague, using my strained and croaky voice, to agree to become my treating physician. They wrote a letter to their contacts, officially declaring me "disease-free." While some of Yaad's foreign colleagues might cry "conflict of interest" from the comfort of their privileged vantage points, navigating such circumstances is rarely straightforward for an immigrant trying to create a better life for themselves and their loved ones. You have to know that networking trumps honest hard work.

In Asian cultures, hard work is mostly appreciated, but ironically, it can reduce the incentive for a company to promote an individual who excels at their current role. The logic seems to be: why fix something that isn't broken? Across both Asian and Western cultures, I've found that working smart is a better strategy. It not only ensures the job is done efficiently but also creates opportunities for one's potential to be recognised in an ethically sound manner. However, working smart alone doesn't always lead to success unless one understands the key players in their environment.

Charisma often opens more doors than hard work without social skills. Take Ted Bundy, for example—okay, bad example—but his charm did get him out of several 'situations' with law enforcement. The point is, charisma can be a powerful tool. That said, there's a fine line between being charismatic and being a bootlicker. True charisma doesn't rely on extroversion or the art of small talk. It's rooted in understanding what is culturally and professionally appropriate, being approachable, and showing genuine respect to colleagues and peers. Yaad would've argued that charisma also requires putting yourself out there—after all, if I hadn't taken the initiative to approach him, our lives might have turned out very differently. Here I am, imagining what others might say, as if debating with Yaad in my own head. Fine, I'll admit it: Charisma isn't about buttering someone up by complimenting how great their brand-new car looks—even if it costs five times their annual salary and is clearly a poor financial decision. Instead, it's about taking the initiative to engage in conversations or actions thoughtfully, respecting boundaries, and avoids stepping on anyone's toes.

Just weeks before I was set to leave, I noticed my chest palpitations had returned. I booked an urgent appointment with Rashida because I was concerned. She ran a few blood tests and glided the ultrasound scanner over my neck. While examining the screen, she asked, "Noticed anything odd lately?"

"No, not really," I replied. "Though I didn't have much sensation in my neck since the surgery anyway. Why?"

She pointed to a tiny, ball-like structure on the screen. "It's probably just your lymph nodes reacting to an infection," she said cautiously. "But as a precaution, let's do a biopsy."

A knot of dread formed in my stomach, but I agreed, giving her the benefit of the doubt. She guided the biopsy needles with the ultrasound, each one digging deeper and more painfully than the last. I winced but stayed still. "All done," she said after a few minutes.

Later that week, I returned to discuss the results. Rashida's face was a mixture of compassion and concern as she said, "The biopsy doesn't look good. This time, it looks different. I consulted a few other doctors, and we think it's more aggressive. We'll need to perform urgent surgery and follow it with multiple doses of radiation."

Thyroid cancers are typically among the easiest to treat, boasting high cure rates. But every so often, a genetically inherited form appears—aggressive, fast-growing, and rare enough to feel like a curse that was likely 'passed' on.

What followed was a painful family discussion about how we could afford the treatments. As a fresh dental graduate in Bangladesh, I barely earned enough to cover rent, let alone medical expenses. Mom was already in debt, and my mamas and khalas were financially drained after supporting *Nanu*'s cancer care. Deep down, I knew the truth: I wouldn't be able to afford the treatment and would soon have to start counting my days.

Desperate, Mom reached out to Aunt Jenny for help. I even offered to write our property in her name indefinitely if she would support my treatment. All she did was "send her best wishes." With no other options, I had to forego treatment.

At that point, I could have chosen to hide the return of my cancer and leave to try and pursue the degree I had worked so hard for. But Yaad's final words kept replaying in my mind: *"Effort is assumed; success is what gets acknowledged. But there's more to life than grinding non-stop for success that others might withhold based on subjective standards."*

I decided against leaving for an overseas degree. As my chest pains, night sweats, and restlessness worsened, I moved to a rural hospital practice near Naria, believing I could do the most good there—for as long as my body would allow me. I should have visited Shiro and Rajesh at least once before I moved, but I kept telling myself I didn't have the time. The truth is, we can always make time for what truly matters to us. Saying, "I don't have time" is often just an excuse—a polite way of admitting we don't want to put in the effort for something we don't value enough.

All I could think of at the time was that working in Naria meant I could visit Mom in Dhaka on weekends and remain closer to "home".

Sufi | Entry 8. All I had

DEAR YAAD,

...

This will likely be my final chapter of confession. I haven't been doing well since the last time I wrote three years ago—the cancer has spread all over my body. But let me start on a positive note.

Mom made an incredibly bold decision. She left her secure nine-to-five job to dedicate herself entirely to something far more meaningful—teaching underprivileged children from farming communities in rural Bangladesh how to write software. Most of these kids had never even touched a computer before. Her mission was to empower them with tech literacy, hoping they'd one day grow into a generation of skilled programmers who could change their own lives. It was her way of giving back, of showing that fluency in English isn't a prerequisite for making a difference; all you really need is a compassionate heart and a clear vision.

I remember Mohfeez *mama* once saying, "People will say your mother sacrificed her life for nothing, gave her best years to people who didn't deserve it. Maybe they're right. But she still sees you as her greatest achievement. Don't let her or her teachings down." Honestly, Yaad, I think her greatest achievement—our greatest achievement—is *you*. Keep shining bright, my friend.

I know a guy who said that Beebo got involved with some shady people and is now on the run from people who want him dead. I wish I could help, but I can hardly get out of my chair these days. I left my dental practice before I could even truly begin. And I'm deeply sorry about what happened to Nida. She deserved so much better.

That's why I've chosen to spend my last few years here in Naria, where I can visit Sammy's grave every day; She deserves better too. Mom has been by my side these past three weeks, and I can see how hard it's been for her to watch her son grow frailer and confined to a wheelchair. She tells me she's here to teach the local children how to use a computer, but I know the real reason she's staying. And for that, I'm deeply grateful.

I thought about calling Shiro and Rajesh, but I think they'll be better off without seeing me like this. Besides, if they were here, they'd probably inscribe my tombstone with *"Here lies Sufi Hamza—he knew a guy."* Damn it, I still don't know what Rajesh's parents do for a living!

Yaad, I know you think I'm some great person who changed your life, but I've done terrible things—things so grave that I can't even say I'll join Sammy when I die. Truthfully, I might be headed straight to hell for some of them. Even so, I'd still want to be buried next to her than in a grand mausoleum like those of the slaver noblemen from long ago! I don't think I've earned an "honourable" grave anyway.

I originally wanted Mom to keep my diary after I'm gone, but she said it'd be too much for her. So, I've asked her to pass it on to you—either after I'm gone or before you leave, whichever comes first. Sorry, Yaad, you weren't my first choice. Not that you'd miss out on much—it's mostly filled with ramblings and nonsense. Still, I want you to have it.

As I write this, I can see you setting up the chessboard on the porch. Thank you for making the time to visit me one last time, and for telling anyone who asked that you didn't know where I was.

This is where my writing ends. They say you can judge a person by what they do in their spare time. But if you have to judge, I'd say judge them by what they choose to do when they know their time is running out.

Thank you for everything, Yaad. I'm looking forward to spending the rest of the afternoon in your and Mom's company, playing what might be some of our final rounds. I've already started hallucinating—I can see Sammy standing in the distance. Maybe it's a sign.

"See you very soon, Sammy."

Yaad | Epilogue

I CLOSED THE DIARY and looked at my counsellor. He stopped typing as I was staring intently. Then, in true cliché therapy fashion, he asked, “So, how did that make you feel?”

I stared at his vague, open-ended question in disbelief.

I glanced back at the hourglass. The clump of sand that had gathered at the neck broke free, and the hourglass began running as it was meant to. It felt almost like time had started flowing again. Then I realised there was more to my counsellor's generic question than I initially thought, but all I said was, “It felt better the second time I read it.”

My counsellor looked at me, now with his pen poised over his notepad, and asked, “What do you think of Sufi's actions?”

This time, I wasn't trying to be careful with my response. I answered honestly, “No one is born evil, but no one is innocent at death either. Sufi did some very bad things, but in my opinion, he never meant to harm any innocents. His heart was in the right place, but his actions clearly weren't. I don't know what to make of it.”

My counsellor scribbled something on his notepad before returning to his typing. "That's quite something," he said. "Would you like to revisit this at another time, once you've had more time to reflect and gain clarity?"

I was annoyed. “Wait, you have nothing to add?”

He looked up from his notes, his face calm. “Counselling isn't going to magically solve all your confusion, Yaad. We're here to listen, to help you process and keep you from making rash decisions. But ultimately, you have to be the one to make peace with it.”

I sighed. “Okay, let me try then...”

I paused to articulate my thoughts before speaking, “What I think after reading it a second time is that Sufi went after people too powerful to face legal consequences—people ‘above the law’. Yes, legally, it was a crime, but morally... I'm torn between supporting him and denouncing him. He wouldn't have had to go through any of it if the legal and bureaucratic systems back home were fair and functioned the way they were supposed to."

As I said that, George Orwell's quote from *Animal Farm* came to mind: "*All animals are equal, but some animals are more equal than others.*"

My counsellor stayed quiet, a small smile tugging at his lips.

I grew nervous and asked, "Our conversations are still protected by confidentiality, right?"

He assured me they were before asking, "So what are you planning to do with the diary?"

"I think I'll hold on to it."

He glanced at the hourglass, half-joking. "Well, our time today is up. Book another appointment if you want to talk, but since you've graduated, it'll cost you."

I laughed. "The only reason I came to counselling was because it was free."

He sighed under his breath. "You and every other student here," he muttered before speaking up again. "Well then, Yaad. I hope you have a good life."

As we stood to leave, I added, "You should throw that hourglass away—it doesn't do the one thing it was made to do."

He laughed and gave me a cryptic response. "Oh, I think it does its job quite well. It stops time on your behalf and lets you think."

I chuckled, knowing he was probably trying to justify a bad purchase he'd made with university funds, using the same absurd explanation he'd offered to everyone else who had questioned it before me.

"You have a good life too, counsellor," I said as I walked out of his office.

That winter afternoon, I stayed at home. I stood by the outdoor fireplace in the backyard, reading Sufi's final entry meant for me—for what felt like the sixth time. My mind swirled with the thought: *Time doesn't stop, and we'll have to move on, whether we like it or not.*

I stood there with the diary for hours before my partner approached from behind and asked the same question my counsellor had just a few hours ago: "So, what are you going to do with the diary?"

I had a very different answer this time. After a moment's hesitation, I tossed the open diary into the flames. The faux leather ignited instantly, and within seconds, the diary was consumed by fire. My gaze remained fixed on Sufi's final pages as they began to burn, my eyes lingering on the words, "Dear Yaad," until they vanished, consumed by the flames along with the rest of the diary...

...

"I'll let the dead rest and leave my past behind."

www.ingramcontent.com/pod-product-compliance
Lightning Source LLC
Chambersburg PA
CBHW051947170626
46808CB00007B/2522

* 9 7 8 1 7 6 3 8 7 7 5 3 5 *